THINGS THEY DIDN'T TELL ME

About Being A Minister Of Music

By C. Harry Causey

THINGS THEY DIDN'T TELL ME ABOUT BEING A MINISTER OF MUSIC
Copyright © 1988 by MUSIC REVELATION

Printed in the United States of America
Second Printing

Illustrated by Sean Isom
Cover and Book Design by Kerry Hamilton
Typesetting and Production by HBH Communications, Inc.

All rights reserved. No portion of this book (including illustrations) may be reproduced in any form, except for brief quotations in reviews and other articles, without written permission from the publisher.

All Scripture quotations are from the New International Version of the Bible.

For further information, you may contact the publisher as follows:

MUSIC REVELATION
7 Elmwood Court
Rockville, MD 20850

ISBN 0-9620795-0-2

Table of Contents

Prelude i

1. They Didn't Tell Me I Would Have to Be a Politician
   The Situation 3
   Some Solutions 13
      Your Serve or Mine? 13
      What Are Friends For? 14
      Planting Seeds and Other Gardening Tips 15
      Can We Talk? 17
      It's All in the Extended Family 18
      A Little Dessert Sweetens the Whole Choir 19
      The Soloist: Endangered Species 21
      Process Is Our Most Important Product 23

2. They Didn't Tell Me I Would Be Married to the Job
   The Situation 27
   Some Solutions 33
      Let Me Ask You Some Questions 33
      Could You Help Me with Something? 36
      Please Call My Secretary 37
      Help! I'm Only One Person! 38
      Happy Holidays 40
      Wanna Go Bowling? 41
      All in the Extended Family 42

3. They Didn't Tell Me I Would Have to Be a Financial Wizard
   The Situation 47
   Some Solutions 53
      Pass the Envelope Please 56
      One More Time — With Feeling 58

The Bonus of Beautifully Balanced Budgets	60
I Love to Count	63
In Spite of What I Said, Here's What We're Gonna Do	65
Such a Deal I Have for You	66
That Will Be $250, Please	68
Misused by Special Permission	68

4. They Didn't Tell Me I Would Have to Be a Psychologist

The Situation	73
Some Solutions	83
And Now, Heeerrrrs Johnny!	83
The Clinger	84
The Complainer	85
The Director	86
The Judge	87
The Turtle	88
The Prima Donna	89
The Florist	90
The Witness	91
The Soap Opera Star	92
Stop, Look, and Listen	95
First You Must Go	99
Stop the World: I Wanna Get Off	101
From Da Capo to Fine	103
Perhaps Your Goose Is Cooked	106

5. They Didn't Tell Me I Would Have to Be a Producer

The Situation	111
Some Solutions	119
Could You Speak a Little Louder, Please?	120
You Light Up My Life	123
Picture Perfect Presentations	124
But I Didn't Know Anything About It	126
Let Me Illustrate	129
Tickets, Please	131
We're Gonna Be Famous	131
Your Place or Mine?	134

6. **They Didn't Tell Me I Would Need to Be a Bible Scholar**
   The Situation 139
   Some Solutions 147
     Inch by Inch 147
     From Genesis to Maps 149
     Bring Forth the Royal Diadem 150
     Quick — What Is Your Phone Number? 152
     Shalom, Shalom 155

7. **They Didn't Tell Me I Would Have to Be a Servant**
   The Situation 159
   Some Solutions 167

8. **They Didn't Tell Me I Would Have to Be an Administrator**
   The Situation 171
   Some Solutions 178
     This One Is Good for the Choir with No Tenors 179
     If This Is July, It Must Be Christmas 183
     File That Under "Inspirational" 184
     I Want Everybody to Know About My Tupperware Party ... 186
     We Need Somebody to Paint the Choir Room This Saturday .. 188
     There's No Place Like Home 189
     Where Were You on the Night of August 27th? 193

9. **They Didn't Tell Me I Would Need to Be a Personality**
   The Situation 197
   Some Solutions 201
     Come to the Party 201
     Look for the Silver Lining 203
     Subscribe to Reader's Digest 205
     Bring in the Clowns 205
     Say "Cheese" 206
     The Shadow of Your Smile 207
     Such Knowledge Is Too Wonderful for Me 209

10. They Didn't Tell Me I Would Need to Be a Disciplinarian
   The Situation 215
   Some Solutions 219
      Here's the Line: Don't Cross It 220
      One Rotten Apple 225
      How Do You Get Into This Outfit Anyway? 226
      I Think I Can, I Think I Can 227

Postlude 231

About the Author 233

Prelude

Being a minister of music was not even on my list. You see, I had never heard of such a thing in the small town where I grew up. One might be a choir director or organist in a local church, but that's what you did as a volunteer. Perhaps, maybe, and even sometimes you *might* receive a token sum for your services. But make a living at it? Never!

The title "minister of music" was itself unknown to me. To be a minister in my home town meant that you were a man who had gone to a seminary, had been ordained, and wore a halo to bed. I knew no church musicians who fit any of those categories. They were all women, they all went to regular colleges for a music degree, and whatever they wore to bed, it certainly had nothing to do with a halo!

Later, when I was in college and graduate school, I knew I wanted to be a professional musician, and I was spiritually drawn to the church and to sacred music. But I quickly learned from my peers and professors that if I wanted to support this young family of mine, and if I wanted to receive *real* respect from the musical community, I would not even consider being a church musician.

So I set out on my journey to be a college music professor. I trained. I learned all about ancient music, analyzed bunches of symphonies, conducted Baroque ensembles, learned to decipher weird looking notation — all in the pursuit of a career that wasn't to be.

You see, the Lord had other ideas for me. Just before I was to step into the world of academia, God caught my attention in a wonderful way. I had a recommitment experience to Him and knew that I wanted to spend my life serving Him in the context of worship and music.

THEY DIDN'T TELL ME...

So the career item that wasn't even on my list rose to the number one position. I became (gad) a bona fide minister of music!

Boy was I glad that I had learned to conduct. I was also pleased that I could lead a choir to shape a beautiful tone, figure out how to modulate at the keyboard, talk to a violinist with at least some credence, and do many other musically related things.

But through the school of experience, I soon learned that there were other "things" — matters of the job that I had not been taught in the halls of higher education. I was in need of help!

Years have passed. Now I am in a position of trying to help other ministers of music through the maze of things they didn't tell us about being a minister of music. It's fun. It's frustrating.

There are lots of surprises in this field. People don't like surprises. Well, sometimes they do — those surprises that add spice to their life and bring some pleasure. But those surprises that jolt us, that cause life to take a twist in new directions, are not always fun.

So I've decided to share some thoughts with you that I hope will help you sort through some of those surprises. If you are an established minister of music, then you will probably already know most of what this book is about to say. But my hope is that you will take a look at yourself once again and find some humor within as well as some practical help that will make this reading worthwhile.

If you are not a minister of music, then perhaps these thoughts will help you better understand the animal that is the church musician. If you're the pastor, you know how much help you need in that department!

Best of all, if you've just begun as a minister of music, or if you are about to graduate and enter this new career — hooray! This book is reaching you in the nick of time. Learn from the successes and mistakes of others before you, my friend, and be equipped for a smoother ride through this crazy life into which God has called you.

What are some of those surprises? Well, they didn't tell me I would have to be a psychologist, or a politician, or a financial analyst. I was surprised to learn that I would need to be a Biblical scholar, a stand-up comic, or an administrator. I went into this field knowing nothing about electricity, but I had to become an electrician on many occasions while I

Prelude

was learning about lighting and sound equipment. I discovered the joys of carpentry while building sets for those wonderful productions.

Some of these areas and others like them require only a slight understanding to get by; but I believe there are certain areas that you will need to almost master if you are going to survive.

Let me tell you how this book is designed. Each section has two parts. The first part states the situation; the second part contains ideas for solutions. The first part will sometimes strike you as humorous and sometimes as pathetic; the solutions portion which follows is there to offer at least beginning ideas on how to make the best of it in either case.

Now let's get something straight: I don't have all the answers. Nobody does. We are in this race together, and we need all the mutual support we can muster. So I'm raising some important issues here, offering some advice which is based on experience, hoping that you will take it from there and soar!

Let me share a sad national statistic with you. The average length of time that a minister of music stays in a job is two years. Only two years! That is shameful. I believe one of the reasons this is true is that many ministers of music have not discovered how to deal with those "things" that this book discusses. Let's change that!

In my work as a free-lance minister of music, I travel around the country and meet many others in this crazy line of work. I correspond with other brothers and sisters who are learning how to unravel the knots in this career choice of ours. I've heard many stories — some funny, some not. And there are often similarities, common threads that bind them together. I want to thank those countless others from whose experience I have lifted many illustrations. Some of you will find yourself within the covers of this book. I hope you enjoy what you read.

As you now enter this gallery of experiences, may you be open to receive inspiration from Him who created the music that we so long to return in worship and praise. Whether you are a volunteer church musician, a career person in this wonderful field, or just an interested observer, may you see yourself — and grow.

CHAPTER 1

THEY DIDN'T TELL ME

◆ ◆ ◆

I Would Have To Be A Politician.

The Situation

JIM HAD BEEN WORKING at a large church in Oklahoma for about two weeks. It was the honeymoon time that all new ministers of music should enjoy.

It was Tuesday night — the night for the Music Committee to meet for the first time with their new wonder boy. Jim and his wife, Marlene, opened their own home to the group. Marlene made her famous chocolate cake. It was to be a great evening for all.

Jim was full of questions. Was the music budget in good shape? Where could he go in this new city to find the best string players for MESSIAH this coming Christmas? Who were the best persons in the congregation to recruit for work with the children's choirs? How often would this committee like to meet?

That was just the beginning of Jim's agenda. Now that he was on board in this new endeavor, he could hardly wait to get some answers from this group of experienced folks.

Everyone arrived. The chocolate cake was a big hit. He knew it would be. The chairman called the meeting to order.

George was a large man. His voice was the type that rang with authority. There was no doubt that he was in charge as the chairman of this committee.

George ran the meetings. That was quickly established. A typed agenda was passed around the room. The group started their work on item after item. Jim waited patiently for his turn. Those burning questions that would set him free to do his job would be answered tonight.

An hour came and went. Jim glanced at his watch. It was already 9:00, and his turn at bat had not come. Then 9:30 arrived. He looked at the agenda and began to realize that they might not finish all the things Chairman George had brought to the committee that night, and only about three or four of those topics offered Jim's desperately needed answers.

Ultimately 10:00 rolled around. "It's time to adjourn," George announced. "But before we go, do you have anything you'd like to ask this committee, Jim?"

Did he have anything? Good grief! Here he was — the man responsible for carrying out the work of worship and music in this church. He had a *million* questions! Maybe *two* million.

"Well, yes. As a matter of fact, I have a long list of things I need to discuss. But I realize it's getting late."

George leaned forward as he responded. His eyes reinforced the tone of his voice. "If you ever want to put anything on the agenda of our meetings, Jim, you need to get them to me in writing at least 24 hours before the meeting. We'll take up your questions next month."

Bubble burst. Honeymoon over. Jim had been baptized in ice water by the one person he had hoped to be his strongest ally in this new ministry.

George, you see, was Mr. Control. Jim was more laid back than that. The church had been so warm in their welcome of him and his family to the job that it never occurred to Jim that he would have to win over the chairman of the music committee. Surprise!

I Would Have To Be A Politician.

* * *

For Sherry, it was not the chairman of the committee that posed the big problem — it was Mrs. Winehart. This lady had been on the music committee for 25 years. Sherry had been in her position as minister of music for five years now, but Mrs. Winehart still saw Sherry as the newcomer.

Mrs. Winehart was particularly interested in having the candles straight, not to mention of the right height. She also made arrangements with the florist for the flowers that were placed on the Communion table each week. They were to be 24 inches high and pass certain other conditions before they were worthy of the Lord.

Sherry was creative. She would like to rearrange the chancel area from time to time and bring in guest instrumentalists. The children's choirs would often stand on the steps to sing, but sometimes Sherry would use risers on the upper chancel level. And then there were the banners.

You see, Sherry wanted to have a special service with lots of banners used in a processional. She had worked out all the details in her mind as to who would make the banners and when. It was to be on Easter Sunday morning, the brass choir would be playing along with the hymns, and a procession of those banners would be glorious.

Needless to say, Sherry's plans did not coincide with Mrs. Winehart's expectations. They had always had Easter lilies in the front of the church, you know — especially on the steps at the front of the sanctuary. Mrs. Winehart's boiling point was rather low. You can be sure that there were some "interesting" discussions in the committee meeting and even more interesting ones on the telephone with other women in the church. There were no banners that Easter. Sherry was crushed.

***

These situations, and many like them, are but small examples of the life of the minister of music in the realm of politics. My father was an amateur politician. I developed a mild distaste for the whole thing. But I rapidly learned that many things in life are political. You give me Boardwalk to go with my Park Place, and I'll let you have all my railroads.

Someone would think that at Creation, God said, "Let there be committees." The world of the church (and the rest of society, for that matter) seems to thrive on them. As you travel the road of worship and music leader, there are many detours along the way. Most of them are called "committee meetings."

Please don't misunderstand me: I do indeed believe that committees are good. At least, I believe that in theory. Sometimes I even believe that in practice. But if I could take back all the time spent in committee meetings and use it for something else, I would probably have an extra year or two on my hands.

One of the reasons those committee meetings are so long is that there is not enough ground work laid. Good communication — that vital, life-giving substance that makes or breaks your ministry — was often not evident before, during, or after the committee's meeting. Good communication is part of the political process. Learn that. You need it.

***

One of my best friends is a minister of music by the name of Mike. He's in a church where the pastor is a practiced politician of the first order — a master manipulator. That's the bad side of politics.

I've heard lots of horror stories from Mike. He'll go into staff meetings only to discover that the pastor has some hidden agenda concerning the

I Would Have To Be A Politician. 7 ♦

music ministry. Other staff members are aware of it, but Mike is the last to know. Right in the staff meeting, the pastor embarrasses him. Questions that require forethought and research are posed in such a way as to make Mike look stupid. He will ask the pastor for permission to do something, and it is not granted.

This pastor spends hours each day on the telephone working through his own agenda with different leaders of the church. He takes them to breakfast and lunch constantly. He goes to their homes at night to work through projects that he wants done. He's a smart man. He knows how to win. And he makes sure that everybody understands that he is in control. Things will be done his way or not at all.

Mike's frustration is obviously high. That's probably why the ministers of music that have served in that church before him have lasted only about two to three years. Mike will probably be looking around soon, unless he learns how to cope with the political animal that is his pastor.

One of the motivating factors of politics is the gain of power. While Mike's pastor is a prime example of that quest, there are sometimes others on the church staff who are running the same race.

***

Doug took the job of assistant minister of music in a large metropolitan church with a growing and talented staff. One of Doug's jobs was to develop a youth choir. The church had long been known for its healthy youth ministry, attracting kids from many neighboring churches as well as its own. But there was just no success in starting and maintaining a teen choir.

Doug was experienced and capable in that area. He had lots of great ideas that had been tested and which he knew worked. The pastor and the chairman of the music committee both gave Doug the right advice. "You will need to clear your thoughts and plans with our youth minister. You don't want to build in conflicts in the kids' schedules."

So Doug set up an appointment with Martin, the highly motivated, successful youth minister. This was Martin's fourth year on the job. He was well known and highly respected throughout the community for his love and nurturing of the teens. He smiled widely as Doug walked into his office.

The smile never left his face, even as he began to throw up wall after wall.

You see, the teen-agers could not be asked to come to rehearsals on Sunday afternoons: That was the time when they had their Team Meetings. Sunday nights would not work because of the church's weekly evening worship service. Monday night was committee night. Tuesday was the teen softball team practice. Wednesday night was Doug's adult choir rehearsal. Thursday night was the teen Bible study program. Friday and Saturday were date nights.

So let's look at after school times. Won't work. There were small groups organized for fellowship; there were evangelism teams being trained to visit other teens in the church and community; there were ski trips and beach trips being planned; and the leaders of the teens were on the planning committees.

Doug was totally frustrated. You name it — it would not fly with Martin. There was no negotiating point. And the chairman of the youth ministry was 100% behind Martin. He already knew that Doug would be coming in for the meeting (Martin had discussed it with him over breakfast the day before), and the chairman had given Martin all the things to say that would make Doug's job impossible.

Martin was "King of the Mountain" with the youth ministry. He was threatened by this new staff member who might steal some of the thunder and affections from the teen-agers. No, the youth choir would have to go.

No wonder former ministers of music had failed to get one started. Now it all made sense. The political machinery had done a great job of being sure the youth ministry was tops in time and money. The music ministry would have to concern itself with other things.

I had a great idea once. At least I thought it was great. I had been working at the church in question for a good number of years and had gained some credibility and respect among the people and leadership there. It never occurred to me that the board of elders would not go for my idea. I just knew they would be as thrilled as I was.

You could have picked me up with a feather after that meeting. They voted no. How could they? I was crushed.

Had I to do it over again, I would not have been so sure of myself. I would have prepared them for the motion that I was making. I would have worked through my committee members and would have communicated with some of the others prior to the meeting where the decision was to be made. That's the political process. What's so sad is that I knew better.

* * *

It's not just with the pastor, the staff, and the committees of the church that the minister of music must become skilled in the art of politics, but it moves into the choir room as well. Yes, among your choir members you will find those whose hands you have to hold. Not literally, of course. That's another subject.

Perhaps the most notorious area for this encounter is the pool of soloists you will have in your choir. Ah, the soloists. Yes, I love the soloists, but many of them need much more love than others.

It was during my first year of college that I worked in a small church near the campus. My first Christmas with the church was approaching. I announced that on Christmas Eve, among other selections, I would either be asking a soloist or the entire choir to render "O Holy Night".

"But that's Frank's solo," I heard ringing through the room.

"Who's Frank?" I dared to ask.

"Oh, Frank is Harvey's brother. He lives in Arkansas, but he comes home at Christmas. He sings 'O Holy Night' every year. Ain't nobody can do it better."

So it seemed the decision was made for me. I was not to pick Martha to sing that solo, even though her absolutely lovely, pure soprano voice was just right for it. Frank, the out-of-town tenor relative, would be here just in time to save the day. He was. He didn't. He sang with a nasal tone. He breathed in the middle of phrases. He sang with almost no empathy, and I discovered later that he wasn't even a believer. But Lord help the minister of music who did not let Frank "fall on his knees" one more time.

***

Being the human being I am (nasty state of life), I find myself liking some soloists better than others. That's doubly true when the style of the music is in question. In other words, Patricia had too much over-the-hill vibrato to handle "Come Unto Him" from MESSIAH. So I chose Doris. Doris was perfect. Patricia was furious. Patricia's husband, Bill, was on the finance committee of the church. Bill was defensive for furious Patricia. When budget time came, I soon realized that I was bickering with Bill over nickels and dimes in the budget. What was going on? I didn't know. I talked to Bill privately later. He was very polite. I probed. Then he said, "Something's going on in the choir. I don't know what it is, but there are a lot of people upset. It seems like you have favorites who always get to sing the solos. I'm not trying to tell you what to do, but it seems to me you'd better take a look at that."

It was so obvious it was painful. Poor Patricia. Poor Bill. Poor me. Had I given Patricia something else to sing in that same service, something written for soprano wobble, perhaps I would not have had trouble with the finance committee. Life is so strange sometimes.

Now what if *you* are a fine soloist? Watch out! I mean, you may be the best there is; but if you are the person who decides who is going to sing the solos, and *you* are your own choice, you are in for jealousy city. That is political suicide!

Perhaps you can't sing solos: You ruined your voice directing choirs. But your wife is an excellent singer. She'll do a great job. Watch out again, buddy: You need to take off your dark glasses before you run into your personal wailing wall. Yes, your wife can and should sing some solos, but take it slow and easy.

***

My wife, Elizabeth, does an excellent job leading children's choirs. So I tapped Elizabeth to lead the Cherub Choir — 1st through 3rd grade. She transformed the group from 10 or 15 whimpering kids into 50 or 60 little angels. Whenever they sang in church, we were led in worship rather than in cute entertainment. The people loved it. The pastor was pleased, and so was the music committee. We were definitely reaching those little ones at a musical and spiritual level that would produce good fruit in the future.

But Anne was not happy. Anne had led that choir in years past. She had done a mediocre job at best. She loved what she was doing while it was going on, but the poor lady communicated like a piece of cardboard and conducted with such rhythmic spasms that I'm amazed the children ever got through a song.

Anne's husband was a big banana in the church. He and Anne invited Elizabeth and me to go out to dinner one evening. It seemed like a great idea at the time — splendid restaurant, good fellowship, a night out of the house. By the time salad was served, their reason for the invitation was clear: Anne was irked. Her musical feathers were ruffled. I had insulted her by not asking her to take the children's choirs, supplanting her with Elizabeth.

It was difficult. The main course was tough, and the dessert wasn't sweet. Politically, I had blundered. Down the road the whole situation caused considerable problems for me.

***

Jonathan serves in a Lutheran church in Virginia. It's a very conservative church both by nature and by architecture.

The time came for the sanctuary to be enlarged. Committees were formed and architects submitted drawings. That was fun and exciting.

As the work was nearing completion, the Decorating Committee was called into action. There would be new paint, some lovely new light fixtures, new window treatments, and — oh yes — new carpet.

It was to be red carpet. It would look great with the wooden pews and pulpit furniture. It would run down each aisle, under the pews, on the steps of the chancel, and in the choir loft.

Jonathan was justifiably concerned about the acoustics of the room. He didn't want the carpet at all; but if there had to be carpet, he would tolerate it only in the aisles — not under the pews, not on the steps, and definitely not in the choir loft.

World War III might be less painful — and certainly shorter — than the ruckus that followed. Few are the churches where the Great Carpet War has not erupted at some point or another. Jonathan needed all of NASA to protect him from the political fallout that resulted! The saddest part of all was that Jonathan was totally surprised by and unprepared for the reactions he encountered to his carpet convictions.

By now I've probably touched plenty of nerves so that you can see the nature of the political bomb that waits to blast the unsuspecting minister of music out of the water. But there is yet another area that I've discovered hiding there, one that I would not have expected would be the source of so much concern. That is the area of small ensembles within the choir.

If soloists can crave more love and attention than the average bear, wait until the not-ready-for-prime-time choir member is *not* chosen for the ensemble. This is the person who is a frustrated soloist at heart — just not quite good enough for the solo part, but definitely better than the average choir member.

You plan to have a one-time ensemble for a special service. Or perhaps you want an ongoing group that can do more and go more places than the whole choir. It doesn't matter whether we're talking about a quartet or a group of 30 voices, this is a select group that will have plenty of fun and get plenty of recognition.

If you just pick the voices you think are best for the group in order to attain a good balance and blend, you are in for it. So you audition. You are still in for it.

You see, it doesn't seem to matter how you go about it — the ones not chosen who really wanted to be in the group will be hurt. Well, not all of them, but somebody will bury deep within a feeling of rejection. Politically speaking, your goose is cooked.

All of these situations will require that you move into the area of expertise in your life called diplomacy. Yes, you will sometimes need to consider your church office an embassy, and you are the Staff Diplomat of the music department. Being a good diplomat is an important part of being a good church politician.

Some Solutions

POLITICS...FEELINGS...POWER STRUGGLES. They are all common to the church, and the devil loves to use them to undermine the true ministry of worship and music that you so long to lead. So if you are going to be effective in doing the things that you so long to do and which you do best, you will need to learn some of the basic skills of politics and diplomacy that go with the territory. Let's explore some of those areas.

Your Serve or Mine?
Develop a servant attitude.

David exemplified it with King Saul. The Apostle Paul lived it. Jesus Christ personified and epitomizes it. What is it? It is the servant heart.

When you join the staff of the local church, you need to take on the role of a servant. You are a servant first of all to the Lord. Then you are a servant to the people, including (especially including) the pastor and the other staff members.

Nobody told me that going from the atmosphere of a professional school of music into the atmosphere of the church music department would be so different. I suppose I realized that I would be moving from a professional level to an amateur level. That's adjustment enough. But I was planning to teach in a college where I envisioned myself as Herr Professor, and I fully expected to be placed on a pedestal and served by the students who would come to sit at my feet. Oh how malicious is the ego.

Becoming a minister of music in the church setting quickly taught me that one needs to get off that imaginary pedestal and learn to serve. Let me encourage you to pray about that — earnestly. If you are like me and countless others, being a servant does not come all that easily. That's the bad news. The good news, however, is that God can grant you a servant heart and the attitudes that accompany it. Pray!

One of my examples in life is a pastor by the name of Ron. Seldom have I met or known a more gifted pastor. He joined the staff of a large church as one of the associates. The senior pastor, who himself had a servant heart, set up a weekly meeting in his office with Ron. At one of the first meetings between these two men, Ron came in and said to the senior pastor, "I believe God has called me here to serve you. I would like to wash your feet."

He meant it. The senior pastor was humbled. The two men embraced. Their relationship was beautiful and complementary. It could have been competitive and divisive. You can fake something like that, but it won't bear fruit.

Nobody told me that I would be asked to come into the church setting and help fulfill the *pastor's* vision — not my own. Ron's example in that was beautifully staggering to me. Let it be an example to you as well.

Get to know your pastor personally. Ask him to put you on his schedule every week — with or without an agenda. Go to breakfast or lunch with him regularly. Share books with one another. Play games together (tennis, golf, swimming). If you can truthfully place yourself in the role of a servant to him, you probably will not have to worry that much about the political issues that will inevitably arise between you.

What Are Friends For?
*Work on cultivating strong,
healthy relationships.*

Who is on that committee with whom you have to work? Get to know them. People are people — everywhere. They all have needs, just as you do. They all have fragile egos, just as you do.

You will find yourself getting a lot more done, more quickly, and with more agreement, if you just spend some time developing friendships with the members of your committee. That's not to say that you should or will have "yes men" on the board. It just means that when they have to say, "No," there will be a higher trust level.

Saying that you *need* to do this and *doing* it are miles apart. How do you accomplish it?

First, I would recommend that you help your committee members realize the need to spend some time in each meeting briefly sharing what's happening in their lives and how they are coping with it. Walls immediately come down when people begin to walk through life together.

Sometimes you will want to take a significant amount of time for this sharing. On other occasions, you can go through it briefly. You may have a meeting where almost all the sharing time is devoted to one individual who is experiencing a major concern in life right at that time. That's good. Focus on that concern and apply specific ministry to it if appropriate. Beautiful relationships in the body of Christ should be the norm, not the exception.

In addition to quality time being spent in meetings cultivating relationships, you need to spend more time *between* meetings doing the same. Have committee members over to your home for dinner. Do with the chairman the same kinds of things you do with the pastor. Have some fun together. Send birthday cards. Call or visit just to see how someone is doing.

If you're going to be really political, you should get to know the family members as well. That sounds like you are doing it for the wrong motives. Hopefully that won't be true. Regardless, you will endear yourself to your committee members, and they to you, when you get to know and appreciate their spouses and their children.

Planting Seeds and Other Gardening Tips
*Learn how to let people know what you're
thinking to avoid surprises.*

How do you win the political games that committees play? Well, you don't always win, no matter what you do; but there are ways to help things go more smoothly than they would otherwise.

One of the first things to learn is seed planting. Like any harvest, it will take time for your seed to grow into recognizable results. But you must not expect a mature crop of fruit to appear overnight.

If you have an idea that you would like to implement, it will meet some resistance if it means change. People are slow to accept change, and that seems to be magnified tenfold in the church. So allow plenty of time and start with planting seeds.

How? Suppose you've decided that you want to take your choir on a singing tour of the moon. Noble goal. In your committee meetings, make mention of the fact that you will be thinking about where and when the choir ought to go on tour at some point in the future. Make it a preliminary thought for the moment. Don't develop it there the first time you mention it, but just ask the committee members to think about it with you for a future meeting's discussion.

Work the moon into your informal discussions with the right people. Get the committee and choir members thinking about the moon. Sing moon songs. Tell some moon jokes. Spread some moonlight around!

Get some literature about walking on the moon and mail it to the chairman of the committee. Just thought he might be interested in seeing this.

Later, after you've planted all these seeds, ask the committee to discuss the whole idea. Don't ask for a decision the first time it's brought up in earnest, but ask for research and thought. Indicate that you would like them to look at all angles of the subject so that a wise decision can be made at the right time.

When the right time comes, when it's decision time, you will then have to let go and let God. Maybe in God's timing this is not the year for your moon adventure. Perhaps He wants you to take the choir to the corner grocery store instead. But at least you will have helped your committee members think MOON before the decision time arrives. It won't come as a surprise when you make the motion that the choir suit up for their space ride.

Now this is going to sound tacky, but it's true. There are some pastors and committee chairmen who love any idea if it's *theirs* — or if they *think* it's theirs. You may have to plant seeds in such a way that the *pastor* says go to the moon instead of you. It's sad that we have to deal with people like that in this world, but such is life. That's where being a patient politician makes a difference.

***

Can We Talk?
Develop the art of good communication.

The world revolves around communication. The most frequent and elementary mistake you can make is not keeping people informed.

Just communicating is not all there is to it, however: You must also develop the art of *good* communication. What I thought you meant is not what I intended for you to hear me say?? Oh well.

What are the tools of good communication at your disposal? Some of them are so obvious that you will feel foolish if caught not using them.

First of all, talk about it. Tell people what you are thinking, what you are feeling, and what you would like to see happen. Speak up at staff meetings. Verbally share with your choir members at rehearsals. Tell the members of your committees what you want them to know.

Next, be sure to make use of written communication. People remember far more of what they *see* than what they *hear*. Write paragraphs or articles for your church's Sunday morning bulletins and for the church newspaper. Allow plenty of lead time, because people don't necessarily read what you give to them the moment they receive it. In fact, it may be next month before this month's church newsletter gets read.

Use posters and flyers. Have some posters professionally printed, or do a good job of making your own. Place them everywhere. Put small flyers into your church bulletin. Mail them out as a self-mailer.

When it's your committee members who need to know something, mail them copies of the minutes of the meeting and also send them letters. Keep them short and to the point so that they will be read. Telephone them a week before the next meeting and remind them that the time is approaching. Inform them about what major items you will be wanting them to make decisions.

Good communication flows two ways. If you are going to be effective and politically healthy in your job, you need to learn to *listen*. Listen to what is said. Perhaps more importantly, listen to *how* it is said. Your goal is to learn to listen for the *feelings* behind what is being said.

Listen with your eyes. Watch posture, eye expression, tension in the lips or on the forehead. You will learn a great deal when you listen well, and it will help you know what you need to do in order to cover your bases.

Part of the whole area of communication and listening is this — It is important that everyone *feel* that they've been heard. When you are working through important, sensitive, or even controversial topics that involve lots of people, find ways that they can *all* be a part of the process.

Let's go back to our former example — maybe you want the choir to go to the moon. Maybe the pastor and the music committee are supportive. But have you asked the choir? Are they going to be surprised when you announce to them that they need to get ready for blast off?

Have a meeting with the choir. If necessary, make it on a special night when you will not have to have any rehearsal. Present the question(s) to them and then get them involved in the process. If they are a large group, divide them into smaller cell groups. Have someone chair each small group — your choir officers, for instance — who will be a reporter back to the larger group. Give them clear, concise instructions and guidelines on how to use the time in the small groups so that they won't spin their wheels. For instance, if you want them to brainstorm ideas on how to raise money for the moon launch, let them know that every idea is valid. If someone has an idea, they should share it with the group. But don't evaluate the idea right then and there, and don't try to act as a committee of the whole to plan the details of any one idea. Just collect ideas — the good, the bad, and the stupid. The best ones will rise to the top, and later you will find consensus among the choir members as they all hear the collective wisdom of the group.

If you are making an important policy decision, it's politically smart to have the choir members represented on the committee that will make the final decision. That might be your choir president or other elected representatives. Make sure the choir knows that they have a representative there, and make sure that they have a means of getting feedback to him or her prior to the decision time.

People need to be heard, and they need to *feel* that they have indeed been heard. In this way, when the final decision is made by the authoritative group, those who disagree will do so in a healthy way.

It's All in the Extended Family
Develop an open, sharing atmosphere within your choir family.

I believe that every church choir should always prioritize becoming a family. That means that at every rehearsal — or almost every rehearsal —

you will spend some time sharing life together.

After a time of opening worship, open the door for the people to share. Or you may prefer to do that before you have a time of worship together.

Ask the leading question: "How are you?" or "What's happening in your lives?"

Some will jump in and easily share all that's on their heart. You will want to give some guidance so that people like that won't consume all of your precious sharing time. Others will avoid speaking up at first, but the day will come when the dam will burst and their lives will overflow with either great joy or great concern. Then they will share. Then they will be extremely grateful that they have a choir family that cares to listen.

Tremendous ministry can and should result from this experience. You may be the source of that ministry, but more often it should come from the other members of your choir.

Becoming this kind of open family — one that laughs together, prays together, and tangibly ministers to the needs of one another — will make for a great group when it's time for your trip to the moon. And they will be more likely to stand by you, even when they disagree with you.

A Little Dessert Sweetens the Whole Choir
*Have each choir member into your home
for dessert and fellowship.*

Elizabeth and I had a wonderful experience with our church choir members with a little exercise we called "CNC" — Choir Night at the Causeys'." Through it we got to know the choir members on a different level than choir rehearsals afford, and they got to know us better as well.

Here's what we did. We took all the names of our choir members and put them into a hat. Well, it was actually a box, but who's looking? Then we drew the names out in groups of five. Elizabeth then telephoned each of those five persons and invited them to our home for dessert on a certain evening, told them to include their spouses if married, and explained that we were having a few other choir members in as well.

If each person were to bring a spouse, our group (including us) would total twelve people. That's a maximum number for what we wanted to accomplish.

After dessert, we informed everyone that we had invited them over just so we could get to know one another better. In order to do that, we wanted each person in the room to share his or her life story. But we had some ground rules.

1. Each person could share as little or as much detail as they wanted, but it had to be done in ten minutes or less.

2. We would move in random order so that each person could share when they were ready to do so. As the host, I would always begin.

3. Each person should include their spiritual history as well as the rest of their life story.

4. Our aim was to be done by 10:00 p.m., so I would serve as a timekeeper for each person as they shared.

It was absolutely remarkable what happened in each of those evenings. We told the groups how their names had been randomly selected, and that we considered each group brought together by God. We tried to make the atmosphere as relaxed as possible, and very few persons were threatened.

There were almost always tears, beautifully mingled with smiles. At the end of each evening, people were hugging, new friendships were formed, and we each had a sense that we were not going through this thing called "life" all alone.

Getting to know one another in those settings not only helped the choir grow as a family, but it helped me with many political situations that came up in the future. It is always a plus to know your "adversaries" when doing battle.

Yes, it took time — lots of it. Elizabeth and I would have to sit down with our respective calendars and look ahead for three to six months. Finding a night here or there that we could dedicate to CNC was not easy; and I admit that there were many of those nights, as I was awaiting the arrival of our guests, I found myself resenting the time commitment. But after each visit, I never regretted a minute spent in that way. Each of those visits produced a warm glow that carried over into the choir rehearsals and beyond.

The Soloist: Endangered Species
*Help your most gifted singers to
practice humility.*

Now we come to that special group of lovable (and otherwise) people who can either be one of your greatest blessings or your greatest challenges. Those who are the soloists need to have some special care.

There is one Scripture that I love to share with the entire choir at retreats or other special occasions and which I like to apply directly to the soloists. It's Philippians 2:1-4.

> If you have any encouragement from being united with Christ,
>   if any comfort from his love,
> if any fellowship with the Spirit,
>   if any tenderness and compassion,
> then make my joy complete by being like-minded,
>   having the same love,
> being one in spirit and purpose.
> Do nothing out of selfish ambition or vain conceit,
>   but in humility consider others better than yourselves.
> Each of you should look not only to your own interests,
>   but also to the interests of others.

What wonderful words for every member of the choir, every member of the body of Christ — the church. But when applied directly to the soloists, and to the potential members of any ensembles for that matter, something happens.

Can you imagine? "Do nothing out of selfish ambition or vain conceit." That would make anyone stop and think twice about "Why am I singing this solo, anyway?"

"In humility consider others better than yourselves." One of the primary things I've heard soloists say is that they thought they could have done a better job on this or that song than the person selected to sing it. Maybe they could. That doesn't matter.

What about "look not only to your own interests." If that last verse were applied by all choir members, there should be far fewer people claiming that "This seat is mine!" I've known new people to drop out of the choir after the first rehearsal just because some long-standing member of the choir insisted on keeping his or her seat on the second row. Your art of diplomacy is needed then, and Philippians 2 can help you tremendously.

Deciding who sings solos or who participates in ensembles requires some type of process. One of the best is to have auditions. If you do, make sure that you are not the only person doing the auditions. When you have to say no, it's politically good to have others there with whom you can consult.

Perhaps it will be just you and your accompanist. Or perhaps it will be you and someone not in the choir who is competent to help. Whatever your arrangement, get yourself out of the position of being the only person to make the choice.

If you do have auditions, be sure to announce them in advance and give everyone an equal opportunity to participate. Yes, you'll have to listen again and again to Millie who has no business singing a solo in the first place, but even the process of auditioning is a blessing to her. Let her sing, if only for a few minutes of your precious time. Your ears can take it.

One method of auditions that I have found useful is to have everyone interested in the possibility of singing a solo this year come on a Saturday morning or Sunday afternoon in the early fall for an audition. These are taped. Notes are kept. When a particular solo comes along, I can refer to my notes and to the cassette tape to select three or four potentials for the solo. I then recall that small group and hear each one on that particular title. In the long run, all feel heard, and you save time.

Process Is Our Most Important Product
*How you do things is often more
important than what you do.*

If there is one thing that stands out in this whole discussion of political considerations, it would be this: Process is our most important product. In other words, *how* you do things is often more important than *what* you do.

Think through the best process you can, outline it on paper, then follow it. You will find two things:

1. It involved good, healthy communication.

2. If you do have problems, it will probably be because you failed to follow one of the basics of good process.

Make sure that the right people — and then all the rest of the people — are included in your process, whatever it is. In so doing, your relationships and decision making are going to go much more smoothly.

No, you don't have to be a candidate for office in order to be a good politician. No, politics are not always bad. There are indeed good politics. Be prudent, and your life in the music ministry will be far more productive for Him. ■

CHAPTER 2

THEY DIDN'T TELL ME

◆ ◆ ◆

I Would Be Married To The Job.

The Situation

MEETINGS, MEETINGS, MEETINGS! Who would have ever thought that one church could produce so many meetings? That is surely the lament of many church staff people — not just the minister of music. And it is safe to say that there are many church laymen who can join in with the sad song, "Show Me the Way to Go Home."

When I signed up with this outfit, they didn't tell me that I would have to be out of the house five, six, or even seven nights a week. Gee, I thought the family was supposed to be one of my top priorities. But it feels like I'M MARRIED TO THE JOB!

One of my good friends in the ministry of music is a fellow by the name of John. He recently sat with me and told me why he found it necessary to change jobs. His case was so typical of the many I have heard (and of my own experience), that he gave me permission to spell it out for you.

John was the minister of music at a church of about 1800 members in Illinois. He was on the staff there for about eight years before moving to another church of about the same size in California.

He tells the same story that I've heard over and over: "The church consumed me! I felt like I would surely burn out if I didn't escape from there!"

Here's John's report. The week began with Sunday. There were two worship services in the morning, and the choir sang in both. He prepared himself for the rehearsals and worship services, checked on the sound system, lights, candles, bulletins, ushers, and all the other little details that went into making the service run smoothly. Then he had a meeting with the pastor in his study for about 15 minutes to double check all the details. That was followed by a 20-minute rehearsal with the choir which was always frantic — not enough time to do all that was needed. And finally the two services. They were back-to-back with about 30 minutes between — just time enough to have another rehearsal with the second service choir.

Home for lunch. Or perhaps lunch out with the family and one other couple from the choir. Fast food, of course.

Back to the church around 2:00 p.m. for the junior-high handbell choir rehearsal, 3:00 for the senior citizens handbell choir, and 4:00 for the high-school choir.

By 5:30 p.m. he was home again for a snack with the wife and kids, but he had to leave at 6:15 to get back to the church and prepare for the evening service.

At 6:40 p.m. the Sunday Evening Service Choir arrived for rehearsal. The service began at 7:00. Home again around 8:45 or 9:00. Too exhausted for anything more, he would still have to help get the children ready for bed. First there were baths, then read them stories, say prayers, and tuck them in.

With nothing left for himself or his wife, John was off to bed. He had made it through yet another Sunday. Monday would soon arrive.

Monday began with breakfast with the Music Committee Chairman. Monday nights were for the committee meetings.

Tuesday nights were for the board of elders, but only every other Tuesday. On the other Tuesdays, John led a small group fellowship at the home of one of the choir members.

Wednesday nights were midweek services and meetings with the choir officers.

There was another breakfast meeting on Thursdays with the high-school kids, and John provided the music. Thursday night was for adult choir and the adult handbell choir which met just before the choir rehearsal.

Friday, praise God, was his day off; but it was the only day in the week when he could find the time to look through all the new music the publishers were sending. So Friday became a day for music research and planning.

Saturday was the only day he could teach his private students. But that was only in the afternoon, because on Saturday mornings he had meetings with his new Worship Team.

And then Sunday arrived once more.

John's schedule also included meetings with the pastor during the week, meetings with the Youth Pastor and Minister of Christian Education (separately, of course), and the regular staff meeting with all the ministers.

He had counseling appointments during the weekdays and sometimes after other meetings in the evening.

He met with the soloists and small ensembles before and after other rehearsals or meetings to go over their special music.

There were two children's choirs, one junior-high group, and a high-school choir, all of which met on weekdays after school.

In his spare time, John tried to keep up with his mail, keep the pianos and organs in tune, help out with the music for the various midweek lunches (senior citizens, young mothers), show up weekly for the junior-high club to play the piano and help with the day school music program for the little ones on Wednesday mornings.

Planning for Christmas, Easter, Thanksgiving, Spring Special, Fourth of July, Annual Revival, and other special events of the church year got squeezed in somewhere. All the while John was overseeing his budget and making sure the bills were paid on time and accurately. It was his job, of course, to place the orders for printed music and other supplies. After that, he worked on recruiting the orchestras for the special events. Then he coordinated the printed programs, posters, etc., that went along with those kinds of things. Somewhere along the way he needed to find time to organize the high-school choir's two-week summer tour.

The church was planning a new building program. John was responsible for helping with the sanctuary and music facilities. That was yet another committee. Their meeting times were not regular — just whenever the chairman was in town. So John had to learn to shift other activities to accommodate.

That was John's normal schedule. Crises just had to be fit in wherever possible. John was a wreck.

John's wife is named Ginger. She's a very loving and patient Mom, but she was finding it super difficult to raise the kids without dad around very much. Ginger loved their church and the people. She sang in the choir, played handbells, and wanted to serve on the new Worship Team.

Ginger was as tired as John, so when the pastor said that the staff would be going away on a full weekend retreat twice a year, it was hard to find enthusiasm. They went, but they were mildly miserable.

Of course the pastor would invite them over for meals. Then there were the special Christmas gatherings at his home and the church picnics.

The choir had those kinds of things, too — an annual fall retreat, a mini-retreat in the winter, and a summer picnic.

Then there was the telephone — the one at home. John thought that it was only doctors who had to be on-call 24 hours a day. Not so. It seemed like everyone wanted to "reach out and touch" John and Ginger. Members of the staff, members of the church, and especially members of the choir would call them for one thing or another at all hours. More than one choir member had called at 2:00 a.m. with personal problems. John occasionally found himself at the emergency room of the hospital or even at the jail at those hours, acting out the role of the Good Samaritan.

Because it just seemed that the family could never escape and have any time alone, John and Ginger bought a telephone answering machine. Boy, was that a mistake. The pastor was furious. He brought it up in a staff meeting, saying that he felt all his staff should be available to him and to the other members of the church at *all* times. He *hated* talking to one of those tape machines, and he wanted John to get rid of it! John didn't. That didn't go over well either.

Poor John and Ginger. They reached the end of their tolerance in that setting. I'm amazed they were able to hang in there for eight years! To regain their sanity, they just had to move on.

Their new job in California is in a church with an entirely different philosophy. No staff member is expected to be out more than four nights a week, and each staff member is *required* to take at least one day off a week, and preferably two.

When John reported this to other members of his former church, they just laughed. "That'll never happen!" they said. It did. John and Ginger are much happier, and they have some time now to concentrate on a much higher priority — their growing family.

John's pastor reminds me of the story Paula told me. She and her husband, Gary, are both on the staff of the same church in Pennsylvania. Paula is the minister of music; Gary is an associate pastor.

The senior pastor believes that all the members of his staff need to be at each and every function of the church. In other words, whenever the church opens its doors, they are to show up.

Gary and Paula have two small children, and she is expecting their third. All of their professional and personal time is directly related to the church. They don't have room in their lives for anything or anyone else, and that's the way the pastor wants it.

This couple has found what John and Ginger discovered: The senior pastor is often a workaholic, and he wants his staff to be the same. Evenings belong to the church. Holiday celebrations belong to the church. In fact, Paula is required to have her choir offer music for Thanksgiving morning services. Since she has to be at the church from about 9:00 a.m. until noon on Thanksgiving Day, there's not much time or enthusiasm left for her to do anything special with her own family.

Then there's Christmas. Not only are there special music services each of the Sunday nights of December, but Christmas Eve and Christmas Day are almost cruel. On Christmas Eve, Paula has three services. There's one in the early evening with the children's choirs. Then there are two identical services later in the evening — 9:00 p.m. and 11:00 p.m. These are with the adult choir, special instrumentalists, and candles. She has to spend from 6:00 p.m. until after midnight on Christmas Eve at the church.

Then, as if there hasn't been enough celebration of the Incarnation, the church has a Christmas morning service at 10:00 a.m. Again Paula (and of course Gary) have to bundle up the children and take them to their second home — the church nursery.

I asked this couple what was the most difficult part of all that pressure. Their response was that among the many stress-producing aspects of their schedule, perhaps one of the hardest was trying to help the grandparents understand why they could never come home for either Thanksgiving or Christmas. Sad.

By the way, both couples reported the same thing: They received only two weeks a year in vacation time, and it always had to be taken in the summer.

***

I've been there. I can personally identify with just about everything these two couples have to say about being married to the job.

My wife, Elizabeth, and I were discussing this situation. She shared her perspective by asking, "I wonder how many wives of ministers of music realize that they will be expected to be on the staff of the church — unofficially?"

You see, the wife (if qualified) is often asked to play the piano, play the organ, lead one of the children's choirs, sing in the adult choir, play or lead handbells, help recruit the orchestra, sometimes play secretary, actually be the secretary on the home telephone, and definitely show up for the church's activities — the normal services and the special ones.

Then there are the committee meetings at her home. She provides the refreshments. She provides the smiles. Sometimes she also serves on the committee itself.

Oh, did I mention the fact that the wife is often expected to do these things without pay? The word is *volunteer*. She is drafted, simply because she is the minister of music's wife. Her pay is *his* salary.

And what kind of salary is that? Well, they vary widely. For most young couples in this line of work, the salary is not enough for them to ever consider buying a house or a decent car. Their income is thrown away in rent and car repairs.

The real danger of all this is resentment and burnout. I don't know why we allow ourselves to get into such situations, but they happen — and they happen very often. We suffer, and the children of such marriages suffer.

Some Solutions

HAVE I PAINTED A BLEAK PICTURE? Well, let me hasten to add some positives. Not all situations are this extreme. Also, there are many, many rewards to serving the Lord — rewards that money can't purchase.

If you are *called* to a ministry, you will be fulfilled in spite of the things you don't like about a job. Everybody can point to things they have to do in their jobs that they would like to see changed. Nothing's new.

But I've shared these scenarios with you for the specific purpose of letting you know what it's like in the arena of church music. These situations are not atypical. What can you do to salve such situations? There are a number of ideas. Let's explore them.

Let Me Ask You Some Questions
Your job interview is an important
place to lay the foundation.

It is customary to have several interviews before being offered a job or accepting it. These will probably be with the Chairman of the Search Committee, with the committee itself, and certainly with the senior pastor.

Interviews work two ways: You should *ask* important questions as well as answer them.

So when you find yourself at that stage now or in the future, remember this discussion about being "married to the job," and ask the right people the right questions.

Who are the right people? Besides those listed above, I would recommend that you talk with all the other members of the church's staff, both as a group and individually. Include their spouses where possible and as many of them as you can.

If the former minister of music is available and, if it is appropriate, include him or her in your conversations. Why did they leave? What were their greatest joys in this job? Greatest disappointments? You will learn plenty; but it will be subjective, so treat it carefully.

There are many "right" questions for you to ask in this process, but be sure that one of them has to do with priorities. What is the top priority of this church? What are the other priorities for its staff?

That's a great question for the senior pastor, but make sure to have him answer it in the presence of others who can substantiate that those priorities are being lived out. Saying that worship, for instance, is the top priority of the church doesn't mean that they act on it.

If they don't say it, you should: Under Christ, your personal priority is to your *family* before it is to your *job*. If they don't agree, don't take the position. If they do agree, ask how this works itself out in practice.

Here are some basics that I believe every church should give to their staff members:

1. Two days off each week

2. Four weeks paid vacation annually, beginning with the first year of employment

3. Normally no more than four nights a week committed to the church and its activities

As for the two days off each week, you might point out that the regular work week expectation for normal individuals is Monday through Friday. Saturday and Sunday are not usually considered working days. Yes, I know, there are many people who work six and seven days a week. Some of them have to; some of them want to. That doesn't necessarily make it right.

At least if you receive two days off a week, you have the option of giving some of that time to the church's activities if you want. And you will — both because you have to at times and because you'll want to.

I Would Be Married To The Job.　　　　　　　　　　　　　　35 ◆

Your work week is Sunday through Thursday. Consider taking Friday and Saturday off. If that is not the best arrangement for you, fine. But two *consecutive* days off are far more beneficial to you, your health, and your family than two separate days. And with two consecutive days, you are more likely to take at least one of them!

Now somewhere along the line in such a discussion as this, you will hear about Sabbath rest. Our Lord created the world in six days and rested in one. We are told that we should take that example for ourselves.

I don't necessarily disagree with that. In fact, even if you are granted two full days off each week, I believe you will either end up working six days or the equivalent of six.

But here is the more important point in question for you and for your peers: Will you actually take a day of rest? Do they grant it and do they *expect* it from you?

You see, some of us almost have to be *forced* to take a Sabbath rest and follow the Lord's example. Most churches will have more trouble getting you *not* to work than they will the other way around!

Concerning the four weeks paid vacation, point out that you are never able to take a weekend here or there as the people in the pew may. You can't get normal holidays either. Also, if your salary level is typical, you are able to earn far more money in the market place than you are in the church setting. Allowing you four weeks of paid vacation is one way the church can compensate you that won't cost them as much money.

When you do take your vacations, and if you get the four weeks, either take them in two blocks of two weeks each or all four weeks at once. You will find that one-week vacations are just not long enough for you to have some mental, physical, and emotional reparation.

Get away. Vacations at home painting the house are fine from time to time, but the telephone will still ring. If you can't afford a beach house or mountain retreat, there are probably people in your congregation who will allow you to use theirs.

As for no more than four nights per week at the church, that's plenty. There are many creative alternatives to your having to be there more than that, and it is *not* necessary for the minister of music and spouse to be at each and every event the church offers.

You will probably run into the objection from some of the very active church members who will say, "But I have a full-time job during the day, I'm here five or six nights a week myself, and I'm not even getting paid for it!" True. There are people like that. But they *choose* that schedule. They are there because they volunteer to be. You may do the same, if you want to. Go ahead. But if you are *required* to be there, it's different. Ask those people how they would respond if their daytime boss required them to also work in the evenings five or six nights a week. Different situation.

Believe me, regardless of how much you negotiate such a schedule or how much you try to keep it, you will still devote 60-80 hours a week on the job. That's the nature of the Lord's work. When He calls, you will respond. Just protect yourself from the heavy expectations that may produce burnout and strain on your marriage.

Could You Help Me With Something?
Learn the fine art of delegating.

Too many people don't know how to delegate. I can identify, because I personally have a high need to be in control. I would much rather do it myself and make sure that I am happy with the results.

"If you want something done right, do it yourself." Right? Well...

There are many, many talented people in the churches of America. Even if you serve in a small church, there are people there who can do many of the things you do as well as you do them. In fact (here it comes), some of them can do those same tasks much better than you! So learn to delegate.

Let's put spiritual language around this. Learn to bring forth the gifts of the people that God has given you. There — I like that better.

What are some of the tasks you can delegate? There are many. Here are just a few of them:

1. Telephoning

2. Graphic work

3. Organizing retreats

4. Planning refreshments

5. Researching robes, music, equipment, etc.

6. Sectional rehearsals

7. Writing articles for the bulletin and church newspaper
8. Hosting a tour group
9. Leading a children's choir or handbell choir
10. Music Library

Get the idea? Making the decision to delegate is the hardest part. Now here comes the next hard part: Keep your hands off of it!

That's one of my greatest problems. I will gladly delegate, but then I still want to keep control of the project. So I check up, scrutinize, and sometimes get involved with doing it myself all over again. Don't do that. If you ask someone to do it, drop it in their hands and expect them to do the job and do it right. Most of the time they will.

Please Call My Secretary
The music department needs a good secretary devoted to that ministry.

Here is another negotiation point in your job interview. Will you receive the services of a secretary?

I was absolutely amazed when I was interviewed for a large church once and discovered that even though they had over 2000 members and a large pastoral staff, only the senior pastor enjoyed the services of a full-time secretary. The other staff members had no secretarial support at all — not even part-time — unless they raised it from among volunteers in the congregation.

A good secretary in the music department is a must. You should fight for your own full-time person, devoted to the worship and music ministry. At the very, very least, you should share a secretary with only one other staff person.

When you do get that secretary, learn how to take advantage of her gifts. She should type all your correspondence. You should learn to use a dictating machine for that purpose. They are much faster and more professional than asking her to take dictation.

Your secretary should keep your calendar, make all your appointments, screen your telephone calls, order the music you've selected, help you with the budget, contact the instrumentalists, oversee the maintenance of the equipment, schedule the use of the choir room and practice time on the organ, and a host of other projects. You should be set free to do the creative things and the counseling — at least as much as possible.

Help! I'm Only One Person!
*Recruit others to help you with
the many facets of the job.*

Many church music programs — even the small ones — need more than one person leading. You should recruit some assistants from the members of your congregation who can help you.

This is similar to the category of delegation, but just a little different. For instance, you can delegate the children's choir totally to a new director. Or perhaps you could best use another accompanist. Those persons become your assistants.

Should they be paid or volunteer? That's a big discussion, but I'll come right to the bottom line. I believe all of your assistants should be paid. Even if the pay is very minimal — a token gift, if you will — it is better to pay them than to use them as volunteers.

Now some people would refuse compensation for being your children's choir director, accompanist, etc. That's fine. At least you offered them something.

Why do I feel that compensation is in order? There are many reasons. The pay increases their accountability to you and to the job. It also helps with their self worth. It is Scriptural. But here is a reason that far too many ministers of music learn too late. The time will come when you will need or want to replace that individual. Reasons vary, but it's inevitable. If they are a volunteer — never having been paid for their services nor even offered any compensation — you are going to have a much more difficult task on your hands. Believe me, the moment money is involved, there is more control over the situation and cleaner lines of responsibility.

How much should you pay? It really doesn't matter. Most people in this category are not doing it for the money anyway. They may in fact contribute all of the money right back to the church. You can pay them $5 a week if you want. Besides, your church music budget probably can't afford to pay them what the job is worth. But when it can, pay them respectably.

If you are a full-time minister of music yourself, then you should consider having an intern each year. An intern is a person who wishes to devote some time — often a year or two — working with you on the job so they can learn what it means to be a full-time minister of music and "follow in your footsteps." They can be a real blessing to you and to your people.

Sometimes an intern is paid a very nominal salary by the church. Often, however, the intern raises his or her own support from friends and relatives. The intern might live with a family in your church, receiving free room and board there as part of their compensation.

Where do you find these persons? The best place to look is at colleges and universities where degrees in church music are offered. Some of them have required intern programs. In other cases, it is the choice of the student to do this for a year or so between undergraduate and graduate school.

Some of my richest experiences in the past were with marvelous interns. I learned just as much from them as they did from me. They had gifts where I had weaknesses, so we were very complementary.

One of my interns had strength in the area of working with junior highs. Hallelujah! I knew the Lord created somebody on this earth who was gifted in that area! She made quite a difference in that aspect of my music program and accomplished things that I did not realize were possible. I learned a lot from her.

Now if you find yourself in a large church, then you might consider having an assistant minister of music join you on the staff. That is not uncommon today, and it is an amplification of the intern idea I just mentioned.

It takes a special person to be a good assistant to you, and it takes special considerations on your part to work with an assistant in the best ways. But the rewards are tremendous.

Volunteer or paid assistants and interns can all relieve you of much stress related to time spent on the job. If you have a spouse at home, then your real marriage may be saved because of them. So treat them kindly.

Happy Holidays
Sometimes you have to find creative alternatives to tradition.

As I mentioned earlier, the minister of music and his family often find their holidays eaten alive. Where there is no remedy for that, you need to look for creative alternatives.

As we grow and mature, we often discover that we can celebrate our birthday on some day other than the actual one. So it is with other special days — Christmas, for instance. The family traditions of Christmas that surround gift-giving, decorations, baking, family visits, and so on, can still happen. They just don't all have to take place on December 24 and 25. Oh, some of them should; but you can plan a family calendar that sees to it that none of these important traditions are short changed.

In our family, especially as our children were growing up, we learned to celebrate Christmas for the entire month of December with an advent wreath on our family table. Many traditions and family worship times emerged through the years. If you have seen my FAMILY WORSHIP AT CHRISTMAS cassette tape and booklet (available through Word, Inc., and through my company, MUSIC REVELATION — see end of this book), then you are already familiar with those traditions. Adopt them for your own family, or adapt them to fit your needs.

Visit the relatives for New Year's Eve instead of Christmas Eve. Open the gifts very early Christmas morning before the church service, or wait until lunch time after the service.

I Would Be Married To The Job. 41 ◆

Whatever it takes, you can find good ways to make the right things happen and give your children fond memories of their holidays with the family. Remember, if there is secure love in your home, and if Christ is the center of your lives, there will be immense positive overflow.

Wanna Go Bowling?
Your social life should not revolve totally around the church.

One of the most wonderful things about being in a good church position is that you establish binding friendships with splendid people — friendships that will last a lifetime.

But if all of your friendships revolve around your church family, and if all of your fun activities are actually church events, you will be limiting yourself in an unhealthy way.

At some point in your life, a bad attitude will creep up on you. You won't feel it coming, so it will take you by surprise. You will begin to tire easily of the church and its demands. You will begin to rejoice when even a fun night with good friends is canceled due to conflicts in weather or

health or some other good reason. You will start saying no to your family when they make requests for outings, even ones that are not church related, just because you are so tired of going out.

These are the first signs of burnout. Just about everyone experiences them sooner or later. But you may take some steps to avoid them.

First, find some outside interests. Discover something you like to do that is not at all related to the church and its various programs. Go to the symphony. Visit the movies. Join a barbershop quartet. Take up golf or basketball or swimming. Have some evenings with the neighbors on your street and play games. Purchase a bike and go riding regularly. Cultivate a hobby such as plants, tropical fish, photography, sewing, painting. Join an investment club and pool your limited resources with others for purchasing stocks.

It's important that your life not be totally wrapped up in the church. You need the change of atmosphere. You will need to talk to someone about things other than church politics.

When the time comes for you to depart this job — and it will — you will find it a little easier to adjust because you will be taking part of your life with you rather than leaving it all behind.

All in the Extended Family
*Your own family will greatly benefit
from a healthy church family.*

In spite of all the things I've said about the all-consuming church activities, let's recognize one thing very clearly. Your family, and especially your children, can and should benefit from the church family. They are an extension of your own family. Enjoy it and take advantage of it.

My next door neighbors have four children of varying ages. One of them is Katie who is about the age of my Debbie. When Katie was around 14 years old, she was invited to a week-long church camp. I was absolutely amazed when her mother told me that Katie might not go. You see, Katie had never been separated from her parents in her 14 years of life, and neither mother nor daughter were sure this was a good idea. I thought that was extremely regrettable, and I was immediately grateful for the experience of my own children.

In the extended family of the church, our children were used to having

I Would Be Married To The Job.

lots of different folks coming through our home constantly. They were also accustomed to spending the night with their friends in other homes. They got to know some other children and a significant number of other adults very well. Three couples come to mind immediately.

One of them was Tom and Norma. Norma was in a neighboring room in the maternity ward of the hospital at the same time Elizabeth was there. Our Debbie was born within hours of Norma's Lisa. The two moms became close friends forever: The two daughters grew up as close as any two girls could be. They spent many nights in one another's homes and learned that not all families are the same. It was a very positive relationship — one that our family has missed greatly since we left that city.

The second couple was Jim and Marge. Marge had a great love for children and an incredible capacity to nurture them. Her own family was almost grown at the time, and the last son was preparing to go off to college. Elizabeth turned to Marge countless times as a new mother to get advice from Marge's years of experience raising her own children. The result was that Marge would gladly keep our David and Debbie in her home for an afternoon, an evening, or a full weekend. Our children loved Jim and Marge, and we loved seeing our own children bring joy to Jim and Marge as well.

Next, I think of one of the other couples on the staff of our church, Mel and Char. They were an older couple who actually became substitute grandparents to our children. You see, their real grandparents lived very far away, as is the case with many couples today. We saw them only rarely. How delightful it was for our two children to have the love and attention of an older couple. Again, they spent the night with Mel and Char on several occasions, learning to overcome any fear of the unknown. Mommy and Daddy always showed up to take them home again.

These are just three examples of many others I can remember. Jerry and Patty, Larry and Ellen, Gary and Karen — many others positively influenced our central family life by sharing themselves with us.

They reinforced in David and Debbie our love for Jesus Christ and the building of His Kingdom here on earth. They corrected our children when they misbehaved. They gave them love and gave them gifts. The benefits of the church's extended family can be enormous, if you take advantage of it.

Now that we are at a different stage of life, I've noticed my Elizabeth doing the same thing for other young mothers. Elizabeth was born to be a mother, and little ones will always catch her eye and her heart. She fondly remembers those years of struggling with diapers, scraped knees, and easily hurt feelings when she received the loving support of the church family to see her through it. Now she can give what she had received.

Before leaving this, I need to say something else. I've painted a positive picture for young families relating to the extended family of the church, in spite of the way the church is often guilty of undermining family life. This paradox is true.

But not every church family is guilty of that undermining, nor can every church family be praised for extending itself to young families.

I learned this by sharp contrasts. You see, I served a church in the Midwest where all the warm fuzzies I've described above are very real. I then moved to another church situation where the opposite was true. In another part of the country, another culture, another style, the people chose to be more private. Being open with one another was just not done. Sharing life was a foreign idea.

Of course not everyone is so cold or isolated there, but most are. I went from what I would characterize as an open, loving church family to one of sophistication, tension, and separateness. It was hard for us. They just don't know what they are missing.

You may find the same to be true for you. You won't change an entire culture or an entire church quickly, but you can be an agent of change. We have to love people where we find them. Gradually, piece by piece, loving relationships can be built.

The sharing of the Christian life is a beautiful experience, but sometimes it takes a lot of work to set it into motion.

CHAPTER
3

THEY DIDN'T TELL ME

◆ ◆ ◆

I Would Have To Be A Financial Wizard.

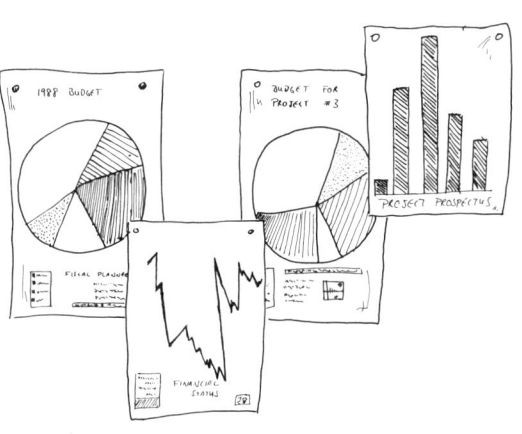

The Situation

MATH WAS ONE OF MY BEST SUBJECTS in school. I actually enjoyed equations and proofs. Some of my friends thought I was weird. They probably still do.

One of the things my parents did wrong was to pay all my bills. If I needed cash for clothes, just ask Mom. If I needed money for a date, just ask Dad. When I went to college, they gave me a checkbook. When I drained the account, the nice guy at the small home-town bank would call Mom and tell her it was again time to transfer some money into Harry's account.

Oh, I worked — both in high school and college. I earned some money along the way to help out, but my parents actually resisted that idea. They wanted me to concentrate totally on my studies and do a good job. I appreciated their desire, and I did a good job. It's just that I also wanted the experience of working in a church music program while in college, so I was able to pay half my way through school at the same time that I studied like crazy. What a good fellow I was.

Having that bottomless checkbook sounds great, doesn't it? Well, it certainly had its moments, and I can assure you that there are times today when I would enjoy returning to that arrangement. But I can now say that my parents did me a great disservice. You see, I never learned the real value of money as a young person, and I certainly never learned to budget it.

Marriage arrived. My Elizabeth had a very different experience from mine. Not ony had she learned to earn and save money, but she had actually lived on her own for some time before we tied the knot. The word "budget" was not in my vocabulary. She had to teach me, and she did a great job.

Before this whole thing is over, I'll share with you some of the basics she taught me and which we have tried to teach our own children. But let's move into the arena of the church with this problem of budgets.

I loved working in the church, and I was grateful that God called me into this ministry. But one of the things I discovered rather quickly was that the pay was not all that great. Now that won't come as any surprise to you, but it needs to be said. I knew that I could make a lot more money if I were to sell insurance, for instance; but that was just not my calling.

I was happy, nevertheless. My parents were not. They constantly nagged me about my income.

"How much are they paying you, Harry?"

"Why can't you afford to buy a car without financing it?"

"When are you going to get a *real* job and support your family the right way?"

"Did you hear about Donald Coleman? He's making more money than you do, and he's right out of college. You've got a *Master's* Degree!"

On and on it went. They wouldn't let me forget that singing for the Lord was no way to get rich. At least the kind of singing I did!

But no problem. You see, the church fathers had a plan for me — a way around this dilemma. When I accepted my first full-time job, they assured me that I would be allowed to teach private music lessons. I could do so using the church facilities and charge whatever I wished. That income was mine to keep.

See Mom! It'll be fine. I'm gonna set up the Harry Causey School of Music right here in the basement of the church. I'll be rich!

Finding students was no problem. Do you know how many people there are out there who want to learn to play the piano? And there are several that want to learn to play it well.

There were also voice students. Most of them were frustrated soloists who wanted me to make them into stars. But bad vocal habits are hard to break, especially if you've been into them for 40 years.

I charged as much for my lessons as the standards of the community would bear. From time to time, I would even believe I was worth it.

The demand for lessons became greater than my schedule would allow. So I found that I had to decide on a maximum number that I thought I could handle. Then I would usually take one or two more than that. You see, I really wanted that money!

I Would Have To Be A Financial Wizard.

And that money was absolutely necessary for us. No, we could not afford a house. No, we could not afford our car. The living room in our rented house went without a sofa until somebody gave us one that they planned to throw out. I remember how we had to set it outside in the sun for several days just to get the smell out, but we loved that sofa.

We weren't poor by any means, but we didn't have much. In fact, one of our favorite forms of entertainment in those days, one we could afford, was going over to the local K Mart some Saturday mornings and listening to the lady on the loud speaker announce the Green Light Specials!

Then the babies started coming. Elizabeth quit work and did her mother thing (for which I will always be grateful). Maybe I'd better take on a few more students.

So I did. "Just a few more scales." "Turn your thumb under here." "NO! That's F sharp, F sharp!" "Did you practice this week?"

That's when I began to realize the cycle I was in. The church fathers didn't think about it either. You see, that income I was receiving from private lessons became absolutely *necessary* for our financial survival. We needed every dollar of it.

But I charged by the lesson. So if a student missed one, or if I had to cancel for any reason, there were no dollars. That hurt!

Add to that the fact that more and more of my time was being devoted to private lessons, yet the demands of the job didn't decrease. Actually, they increased. So I found myself in more and more trouble with time, getting more and more tired as I went.

Then taxes became a reality. They have a way of doing that every spring, you know. That income from private teaching represents self-employment. Nothing was withheld. I had not set any of those precious dollars aside to cover that inevitability. Guess I'll just have to take in one or two more students so that I can afford the taxes next year.

ARRGGH! Somebody get me off of this thing! I felt trapped.

As I thought through the situation more, I began to get angry. Perhaps my anger was wrong, but I was angry just the same.

At whom? At the church fathers. You see, there were ten ministers on that staff. Ten. Each received a pay package — base salary, pension, vacation time, etc.

When I compared mine with theirs, some lights came on. I had been there for several years, yet I was the lowest paid person on the staff. That's typical for the position of minister of music, you know. Besides that, I had no pension plan, and I didn't get as much vacation as the others. Not fair.

So I went to the church fathers. I complained. They listened, but they didn't like what they heard.

"You don't deserve a pension plan," they answered. "You're not ordained." It was the same with the vacation time and the salary.

You want to know what was sadder than their saying that? I believed them. I really felt I was unworthy of being cared for like those guys of the cloth. My self esteem went down. I was *just* a minister of music. They didn't tell me that I might feel this way — or why.

I guess I'll just have to take on a few more students.

Then Gary came on staff. I love Gary for many, many reasons; but the first one I had is that he was not ordained either. Yet he received a larger salary than mine, one more week of vacation time, and a pension plan.

I Would Have To Be A Financial Wizard.

Aha! If I don't deserve it, neither does he! Or the other way around. If *he* "deserves" it, so do I!

The church fathers had to rethink the whole thing. They agreed that they had made a mistake. The situation was rectified, and I was much happier as a result.

But you know what, there remained in the minds of some of those men a resentment towards me. In their minds, I was greedy. I was building my own kingdom, and I was in love with money. It hurt.

If my own personal budget was a challenge, you should have seen me trying to deal with the church's budget in the area of worship and music. They actually expected me to make annual financial predictions for the coming year and present them to a committee of businessmen in three-piece suits. Then they expected me to keep track of all my expenditures, justify each one, and not spend more than they told me was allowed.

Oh Mom and Dad, could you please send a bottomless checkbook to this church?

Well, I learned as I went. I know what I'll do: I'll keep a notebook. I'll list a column for each budget item they tell me I have to track. Each time I get a bill, I'll write it in that column, adding them up as I go. At a moment's notice, I'll be able to tell how much I've spent in this or that category. By comparing it with the amount allowed at the top of the page, I'll be able to see how I'm doing.

Great idea. It really helped. Then the financial secretary of the church sent out the monthly statement to me. Her figures didn't agree with mine. *She* must have made a mistake.

I met with her. We had to pull out invoices from folders all over the place. How could anyone keep track of so many invoices?

We compared. Thank God for calculators! Her figures were right. I had failed to note a few bills, and I had added several columns wrong. (Didn't use a calculator.)

As I began to get my act together more in the area of accurate record keeping, the budget year moved on down the road. Summer passed and fall came racing towards me. Time to order all the new music for the fall. That was perhaps one of the most exciting times of the year for me — the arrival of the new fall music. I loved introducing gem after gem to the choir and watching their enthusiasm build for this piece or that.

But the price of music had the audacity to go up from what it was just a few years ago. These bills were larger than I thought. And the choir had grown, so I had to order more copies than before. And when we repeated some of the old music, there weren't enough copies of those either. So I had to order some more.

Christmas was coming — the busiest and best time of the year for church music. Well, all would agree that it's the busiest, anyway.

Time to order the Christmas music. Then the moment of truth came: The money was just about gone. There wouldn't be enough this year to hire the orchestra for MESSIAH. In fact, I wonder if we can even afford to buy the scores? Frustration.

What could happen next? I'll tell you. A little memo came around to all the staff people from the church administrator.

> "Due to a downward turn in giving patterns, we are running behind budget. All departments are asked to cut all spending immediately until this situation changes."

What?! Do they expect me to make bricks without straw? Don't they realize that Christmas is coming??

So I met with the church administrator. "Don't you realize that Christmas is coming?" I asked with a pleading in my voice.

"Yes, praise the Lord, I do. You see, the giving always seems to drop in the summer. It picks up a little in the fall, but barely enough to get us over the summer slump. But people always make larger gifts at Christmas time. End of the tax year, you know. So we'll probably pull out of this by December 31."

December 31? But the Christmas concert would be about three weeks before that! What was I to do?

Well, we made it. No panic was necessary. But I panicked anyway. Felt good. Felt awful.

Through that process I learned bunches about the church budget process, the cutbacks that happen like clockwork, and the need to plan, plan, plan ahead.

Well, the time came for submitting the facts and figures by which the budget committee of the church would be making the decision about the amount of the music budget for the following year. What a relief! I was so glad at what I had learned and that I would be able to ask for more money next year. Things would go much more smoothly now.

I submitted the figures to them and made my request for the next year. It was a very conservative budget as far as I was concerned, but it did give me the increases I would need to keep things on course.

My bubble was burst — they rejected it. I couldn't believe it! I had been absolutely honest in what it had cost me and what I needed to continue, but they gave me several thousand dollars less than I needed.

Yet some of the other departments of the church got some pretty nice increases. I remember some of the other staff members basking in the glow. I was jealous. Why didn't they like me? Wasn't I doing a good job?

It took me years to answer that question. Yes, they liked me. Yes, I was doing a good job. So what was wrong? I was not asking for the needed funds in the right way. I gradually learned different ways of doing things, and matters improved. I'll share them with you later.

One of the things I discovered the hard way is that the church in general often operates on the philosophy that "cheaper is more spiritual." The unfortunate result is a reputation of mediocrity.

Well, the personal income problems and the church budget process didn't make me into an overnight financial expert. That's the wrong field for me. But my eyes were opened, and I discovered the great need to become financially astute. Maybe some of what I learned will help you.

Some Solutions

ONE THING I HAVE NOTICED ABOUT MYSELF and 99% of the other folks I know in America, a feeling of positive self worth is often tied to your income or lack of it. When we have money in the bank, we feel good about ourselves; when we have more bills than income, we feel like rotten turnips.

That's understandable, but we need to be reminded that the Lord does not work on that philosophy. Remember what He said in the Sermon on the mount?

> Do not store up for yourselves treasures on earth,
> where moth and rust destroy, and where thieves break in and
> steal. But store up for yourselves treasures in heaven, where
> moth and rust do not destroy, and where thieves do not break in
> and steal. For where your treasure is, there your heart will be
> also.
>
> No one can serve two masters, Either he will hate the
> one and love the other, or he will be devoted to the one and
> despise the other. You cannot serve both God and Money.
>
> Therefore I tell you, do not worry about your life,
> what you will eat or drink; or about your body, what you will
> wear. Is not life more important than food, and the body more
> important than clothes?
>
> So do not worry, saying, "What shall we eat?" or "What
> shall we drink?" or "What shall we wear?" For the pagans run
> after all these things, and your heavenly Father knows that you
> need them. But seek first his kingdom and his righteousness,
> and all these things will be given to you as well.
>
> *(Verses selected from Matthew 6)*

Yes, we know these verses, but we must recommit ourselves to them repeatedly. If we don't, we will find ourselves caught up in the world's system.

There's nothing wrong with having money. Money is not evil; it's our *attitude* towards it and our *use* of it that are often brought into question.

I publish a monthly newsletter called MUSIC REVELATION. I do make a profit on that endeavor, but my expenses are so great that the profit is only a snap of the fingers.

I received a nasty letter from someone in my city questioning me about all sorts of things in my professional and spiritual life. I arranged to meet with this lady and her husband at a restaurant to discuss her concerns.

It was a beautiful meeting where mutual understanding and healthy communication resolved many misconceptions.

But at the end of the meeting, she asked me one final question, "Harry, is it true that you make $350,000 a year on your newsletter?"

My immediate reaction was a burst of uncontrolled laughter. I couldn't

I Would Have To Be A Financial Wizard.

believe my ears! Surely she was joking!? But I looked at her expression and immediately realized that she was deadly serious. This was really under her skin.

"No! Absolutely not!" I told her. Then I proceeded to divulge my personal financial picture which — believe me — was miles and miles away from her question (accusation). I was used to being open about my finances since I had worked in churches where everybody knows what you make and pretty much what you do with it.

After I had satisified her curiosity, however, I added a question of my own. "But what if I did?" I asked. "What difference would it make? If God chose to give me a *million* dollars, and if I chose to give all or most of it away for His purposes, wouldn't that be His choice and my business — not yours?"

Having money is evil in the minds of some people. Not so.

Working in the church music ministry will not make you wealthy, so you must learn to make the most of what the Lord gives you. That's where Elizabeth helped tremendously as she taught me to budget our personal income. That discipline also helped me in the area of managing the church's budget.

If you — no, *when* you find yourself needing financial help and guidance, there are always people in your church (perhaps on your staff) who can help you. Take advantage of that. If you have to humble yourself to do so, it won't hurt you.

First and foremost in your personal financial life, you should tithe. God commands it. He expects it. He will honor your financial rewards if you honor His principles.

I believe you should tithe the gross income, not the net. And I'm talking about a full 10% of the gross. Some people set a figure less than 10% and call it a tithe. It's not.

Anything you give over that 10% constitutes your offerings to the Lord. So if you want to give gifts to His work, you need to be setting aside at least 11% or more of your income for that purpose.

Don't ever say that you can't afford to tithe. You can't afford not to! The Lord is your eternal banker, and He will bless you for your obedience.

Next comes the habit of saving. Ideally, I believe you should match your tithe amount with a like figure that you place in a savings vehicle never to be used unless in an emergency. The earlier you establish that habit, the better you will be. Teach it to your children — diligently.

Pass the Envelope, Please
Learning to budget your personal finances is freeing.

One of the first things Elizabeth taught me in our financial life was what we called the "envelope system." We still do it today, even though it is not always necessary.

With this system you decide what small areas of your life will be on a cash basis. Ours included such things as the barber, dry cleaning, food, hobbies, and entertainment. That last category had to do with getting a pizza instead of cooking in, or going to the movies instead of watching television.

You could certainly add any number of things to that list, such as clothing allowance, gas for the car, gifts, whatever.

Each month, when the pay check came, we would convert some of it to cash and put the agreed amounts in those various labeled envelopes. Carefully tucked away in my desk drawer, those envelopes were a real blessing. If the money was there, and we wanted to do it, we did. If the money was not there, and we wanted to do it, we didn't. That was the key — self-control. The envelope system gave us a visual clue as to the state of our financial affairs, and we learned self-control along the way.

Yes, we would sometimes cheat. But it had a way of catching up with us, and we never felt good about it. You can rob Peter to pay Paul only so much: Peter will go broke.

The biggest problem that came along was plastic money. It was too easy to get charge accounts and use those cards as if we could afford the things we were buying. If you have never been caught in that snare, consider yourself blessed. Don't do it!

You should, I believe, have at least one major credit card. There are some things in life you can't do without it. But you must never allow yourself to charge items you are not able to fully pay for on a month-by-month basis.

Learning to budget for monthly expenses goes beyond the envelope system. You need to sit down and write out each and every fixed expense you have. Make estimates if you don't know for sure what a monthly bill will be. Add them up. How much will you need to make your obligations each month? Now how much is left over? That's what you may spend, give away, and save.

I Would Have To Be A Financial Wizard.

Budgeting your personal income, large items and small items, is much like that simple envelope system. Just figure out how much needs to be in each category, put it there, and don't spend it for anything else.

* * *

Ernie was a member of my choir and a good friend. I could tell that something was wrong, however, because he wasn't joking as much as usual, and his face looked long and worried.

"What's wrong, Ernie?" I asked. "Don't you feel well?"

"Oh, just a few problems at home. Nothing serious. Everything'll be fine."

I didn't let it go there, however. "Let's go to lunch this week. I'll buy. It's been a while since you and I caught up."

"OK. I'll call you," he replied — but somewhat reluctantly.

We met. We ate. We engaged in some small talk. Then the truth came out. Ernie and his wife were fighting. They were fighting over money. Very common problem in marriages. They were living beyond their means and didn't know how to get out of the situation.

Ernie was embarrassed to share this with me. His feeling of self worth was about as low as it had ever been. I knew how he felt, because I had come through the same valley during recent years.

"Ernie, I believe I can help you. Will you let me?"

"But I don't want to bother you, Harry. Besides, you don't have enough money to help us."

"I wasn't referring to giving you money, Ernie — although we might be able to do something like that through the church. What I meant was that I would like to share with you some budgeting ideas that will help you and Margaret learn to manage the money you do have. And I'm willing to shepherd you through the process. But it means that you and Margaret will have to do this together, and you'll have to trust me with private information about your income and debts. Are you willing to do that?"

His answer was yes, but he would first have to talk to Margaret, of course. It isn't easy to humble yourself and allow someone else to know the details of your private checkbook, your needs, your wants, and how much money you *don't* give to the Lord's work — even though you know you should. I was proud of Ernie and Margaret for being that transparent with me, and I was grateful that the Lord had equipped me somewhat to be a servant to them in this category of their lives.

We met a number of times. I put them on the envelope system and helped them decide how they could pay off their debts — one by one — and how long it would take.

The first thing of which they had to be convinced is usually the biggest stumbling block of all. They thought going onto a budget would be limiting. Instead, it is *freeing*. Rather than worrying about where the money is to come from to pay certain debts, you know exactly where the money is and that there's enough. Of course, you have to alter your life habits, and that's a real challenge for young and old alike.

Ernie and Margaret didn't have an easy time of it, but they did make it through. They rejoiced when they could see the light at the end of the tunnel, and they truly celebrated when they finally got out of debt.

You may find yourself in similar circumstances either now or in the future. If so, remember Ernie and Margaret's example of humility.

One More Time — With Feeling
Giving private lessons on the job can work, if you're careful.

Remember the interview process we talked about earlier? Well, when you interview for a job, and if they tell you that you will be allowed to teach private lessons for extra income, turn them down.

Explain that it is important that the church be willing to support you adequately and meet your family's needs without your having to depend on giving private lessons for income. Tell them that you want to devote all of your time and creative energy to doing the job for the church — and doing it right. If and when you are well established, when a good foundation has been laid, you might consider taking on a few students. But even then, you would want to concentrate on those who will be offering their talents back to the church in worship and music.

All of that is designed to help you avoid the trap I described above. With just a little logic, those who are doing the interviewing should understand and appreciate your stand on the matter.

Now that doesn't mean that they will automatically pay you more money — at least not more than they had already determined their budget would allow. But it may very well help them with their criteria in giving you the largest salary they feel they can afford, and it may help with future raises.

So start the job without private students. If you need or want to give some voice instruction to some special people in the choir, go for it. Just don't meet them more than three or four times, and don't accept any money for those lessons. Explain to them that some day you may be able to work in some private lessons on a regular basis; but for now, this is just a temporary thing.

Down the road you may be ready to teach students. If so, let me give you some advice. Wait until you have yourself well organized with assistants (paid or volunteer), secretarial support (full-time or part-time), plans laid out for the next five years (at least in general), and your calendar such that you are sure your family is not being short-changed. Then you may decide how many hours a week you are willing to devote to private lessons.

If you do take on students, here is another very important principle for you to adopt. Don't take the extra income and use it for your normal living expenses. Don't use it for entertainment, either. Well, maybe some of it; but very little. You see, the moment you do that, you will begin to *depend* on that income. Your standard of living will rise slightly, and you will become so used to it that you will feel you just *have* to have it.

Remember that this income will not be steady. People will miss lessons. Some students will drop, and you will suddenly find yourself losing a significant amount of income monthly. So don't count on spending it.

Instead, take that extra money, tithe it, perhaps take a percentage of it out for fun and put it into your entertainment envelope (oh boy, more pizza next week!), and then save the rest. That's right, put it away. Having enough money to save is going to be one of your biggest problems. This may be one of the solutions.

Save it in some way that it will work for you. Put it into mutual funds or into an IRA. Just remember that your tax liability will increase because of that extra money, so you should keep some of it liquid just in case you need it to give to Uncle Sam.

If you can arrange it, give the lessons at some time other than your day off. You need that time. Your family needs you. Preserve that time selfishly, because nobody else will.

The Bonus of Beautifully Balanced Budgets
How to make the church worship and music budget work.

How much money should the church set aside for the church worship and music budget? Good question.

I believe that worship is the top priority of the church. No debate. After all, when Jesus was asked, "What is the greatest commandment?", He didn't say "The pulpit." Nor did He point to evangelism, missions, Sunday School, buildings, youth ministry, Christian education, or even music. He said the greatest commandment, simply put, is to love God!

That settles it. The top priority of the church is to love God. Granted, we do that in a variety of ways; but the primary way, I believe, is through worship.

I'd better not get off on this subject any more deeply. Those of you who know me know that I could write or talk about this until next year's crop comes in. So let me just say it and go on.

In the corporate worship setting, how do we most express our worship to the Lord? Through music. I believe that music is the greatest gift God has given us to worship Him — bar none. God has shown us in the Bible that He reveals Himself through music that is offered to Him in worship.

Here I go again. That's another of my favorite topics about which I've taught for years. So let me leave that topic, too, and move on.

If worship is the top priority of the church, and if music is the greatest gift

I Would Have To Be A Financial Wizard.

God has given us to worship Him, how important ought the worship and music budget of the church be? Another good question.

Not that the amount of money budgeted for your program should be the largest budget for the entire church, but why not? Love God with *all* your heart, soul, mind and strength! That just might call for greater financial support for the worship life of your congregation than originally thought.

As a general rule of thumb, I believe that a local church should budget a *minimum* of 10% of the total church budget for worship and music. Yes, I'm including salaries in that figure, but only the salaries of the church musicians — not the pastor's salary. He is a special category unto himself.

If you church's annual budget is $300,000, your annual music budget should be in the $30,000 range. I've seen many, many churches with annual budgets in the $750,000 category and higher, yet the music budget is still around $30,000. Tragic.

Keeping track of the budget you do have is essential. Setting up a notebook as I described is one way to approach the situation, and it is indeed helpful. But in this day and age, that's considered "horse and buggy." You ought to move up to a computer. That's right, a personal computer for the music department.

A basic computer is not all that expensive any more, and with it you can keep track of all your music, all your equipment, all your personnel with the thousands of bits of information you need on them, all of your worship bulletins, all of your correspondence, and — yes — all of your music budget.

You can make annual projections on how much things will cost. You can spit out on your printer exactly what you have to spend right now and how much you've already spent in any category. That's a huge time saver for you, and it gives splendid reports to folks who are impressed by those kinds of things.

Have you ever heard this — "GIGO?" It's a new phrase in our vocabulary, and it's already found its way into the dictionary. It stands for "garbage in, garbage out." It simply means that if you put dumb information into the computer, it will obligingly spit out dumb information.

So you have to learn to use the computer and the various programs that come with it. No big deal. If you are not yet "computer literate," and if you are scared of those things, don't feel lonely. Lots of folks are in the same bag with you. But believe me, learning the basics of the computer and working some of the friendly programs that are available to you for church music ministry management will be no problem. If you can conduct a choir or orchestra, that's much more challenging than learning the computer.

So don't let this marvelous tool pass you by. Get on board with the way things are done today — and survive.

Regardless of whether you choose to remain "horse and buggy" or whether you move to the space age, you need to keep accurate records. Simple. Just do it. They taught you to add and subtract in the first grade. By now you should be pretty good at it. Just plan on disciplining yourself to keep a written record of all your expenditures in the music budget and be able to give an accounting of each and every bill.

You say that the church has a financial secretary who does that? Great. But you should keep your own books for your particular area of responsibility and know at a moment's notice how things stand. Don't bug him or her with questions that are your responsiblity.

In keeping these kinds of records, you are going to be equipped to do a dynamite budget presentation for next year's requests.

I Would Have To Be A Financial Wizard.

I Love to Count
Making an effective budget presentation will increase your budget.

The subtitle of this section may be a bit strong. Maybe there is no guarantee that making an effective budget presentation will absolutely and assuredly bring about the desired result of a larger worship and music budget, but I can say with certainty that it will help greatly.

You see, those guys (excuse me, ladies — those persons) who do the budget analyses and projections, those persons who will decide whether you get what you are asking for, are usually of a certain personality type. You know what I mean. They *love* numbers. Most of them are businessmen in real life. Some of them are highly successful ones, too. Those are the types of people to whom the church looks for formulating and dispensing the total budget.

You know what they love as much as numbers? They love detail. Give them highly detailed information, and their chimes ring.

So when you want them to know that you need $250 to buy printed music for next year, you've got some convincing to do. Prove it.

Here's what you share with them. If you can do it with pie charts and bar graphs, they'll be even more pleased.

Let's pretend that the average cost of an anthem is ten cents today. Boy is that pretending!

How many anthems does your choir sing in a year? Have you ever tried to figure it out? You might be surprised.

Let's say that your choir only sings an anthem on Sunday morning 52 weeks a year. Let's see, 1 x 52 = 52 anthems. I believe I'm getting the hang of this.

But the choir sings two anthems on some special days, such as Thanksgiving Sunday, Easter Day, Christmas Sunday, etc. Better add in about six extra anthems to be safe. That brings us to 58.

Now the same choir also sings in the evening service twice each month. When they do, they sing two anthems. That's 24 titles per year on the average, bringing the total to 82 anthems a year.

But wait. What about the special Christmas service. Goodness. We sang 12 anthems in that last year. Or perhaps you sang a cantata instead. There's still an extra cost involved. If you add 12 Christmas anthems to the regular Sunday morning and Sunday night collection, and if you remember the Spring Special, the Fourth of July celebration, the annual Revival, and so on and so forth, the grand total rises easily from 82 to 100. I don't know where your total would be, but you understand the process.

If your total is 100, how many of those are new titles, and how many of those are repeats? Well, here's an area where people vary widely. This is subjective, but I believe that it is very vital to keep new and fresh music flowing through the choir at all times. How much new and fresh music, you ask? I don't know. But for me the rule is around 75% new music.

That brings the total of new acquisitions down to 75 per year rather than 100. But there is also the children's choir music, the quartet music, the ensemble music, the handbell music, the trumpet trio, the ladies trio, some solo literature, wedding music, memorial service music, and you-name-it music. With no problem at all, the total is back up to 100.

Multiply that by the average fictional cost of ten cents, and you come to an annual cost of ten dollars for new music. But that has to be multiplied by the number of copies required. How many did you say you have in your choir? Did I hear you say 25? (That's considered the national average, in case you'd like to know.) Well, the cost just reached $250 per year — your targeted price.

Now if you stayed with me through this ludicrous and tedious example, you can see that all this detail (going around the barn if you will) gives supportive evidence to your budget requests. You didn't just get the numbers by going into your closet to pray about them. You have — here it comes — *statistics* to back up your requests.

The budget committee will love it. You just pushed their button. Why it has to be that way, I don't know. But then again, does it really matter why?

In Spite of What I Said, Here's What We're Gonna Do
It's important to have a Plan B when cutbacks occur.

In spite of your careful budgeting and the granting of your visionary requests for music, there will come times in the church's life when giving will not keep up with the hopes and expectations. It happens in the best of churches.

What do you do about that? You have a Plan B.

Yes, I know you wanted to hire the local symphony orchestra to accompany the Christmas musical this December, but you can't afford it this year.

What now? You use the taped accompaniment. What do you mean you never used tape accompaniments? Some of them are quite nice — much better than your local symphony.

Oh well, if you are going to be that way, then you'd better have a Plan C: You're gonna need it.

If you planned to do MESSIAH this year with Baroque orchestra and a taped accompaniment is out of the question for you (is there such a thing as an accompaniment track for MESSIAH?), then you'd better know that you have accompanists who can back you up at the keyboard. That's your escape route. Or you'd better have a different musical selection in your back pocket — always. You can certainly take some of the choir's favorite Christmas anthems from this year and former years, group them together by caegories such as prophecy, angels, shepherds, and that sort of thing, read some appropriate Scriptures and other readings, have a child soloist, light some candles, and no one but you will know that MESSIAH was not offered here this year. Perhaps no one but you will really care.

Such a Deal I Have For You
*Being a good steward of your budget
will stretch it further.*

If you are serving in the average church, your music budget will not be as large as your vision! If it is, maybe you'd better examine your vision!

When this is the case, you shop for bargains. That's what you have to do with your personal funds, isn't it?

I've made a number of pilgrimages to Israel. One of the things I love to do there is shop, because the cultural tradition is that you never pay the asking price. You always bargain.

It's fun to play the game. I've known the asking price to be $150 and yet get the item for $10. In fact, I've twice seen valuable items (one $150 and the other $300) actually *given* away by the shopkeeper — no money exchanged. It's a crazy world outside of America. Come to think of it, America's not so sane, either!

If you've been to Mexico and other places where shopping bazaars are common, then you are no stranger to bartering and bargaining. But someone has told us that you don't do that in America. Wrong.

Paying retail for anything in this country is because of laziness. This country is based on free trade and competition. If you are willing to do the work, you can bargain for almost anything — or at least find places that will sell it to you for less than retail.

If printed music is the item in question, you only have to pay full price for it if you want to. Perhaps you have a favorite music distributor who gives you excellent service, but he charges you full price or only gives a 10% discount. Pay it if you wish. That kind of relationship is worth something: Excellent service is sometimes more valuable than saving a few dollars. But there are other ways.

There are many music discount houses who regularly sell music for 20%-30% off the retail price. And many of them also give great service. It's a free country, and you can use them instead. It will save you lots of money in the music budget.

Also, don't forget that you can purchase music directly from the publisher. They don't usually advertise that fact, because music distributors get uptight with the publishers for doing that. To keep good business relationships and peace in the family, the publishers keep quiet.

But sometimes you can get faster service and better prices right from

I Would Have To Be A Financial Wizard.

the publisher. If the item you are seeking is an older publication (by that, I mean several years old or more), and if you can honestly say to the publisher that you are having financial difficulty, they are often very willing to give you great deals. I've known publishers to sell collections that retailed for around $5.00 for only 25 cents per book.

Granted, those were very special circumstances; but you never know unless you ask. If you do get such special treatment, I believe you owe it to the business involved to place future orders with them for regular prices.

Music is not the only item for which you should shop. There are many others. Here is an example.

I was getting ready for a major musical presentation in our church. It was going to be expensive, so I was looking for ways to cut the cost as much as possible.

One of the major costs was for the printing of the special program. I wanted a particularly expensive paper that would have to be ordered by the printer.

So I pulled out the yellow pages and discovered that there were many different paper distributors in town. If your location isn't large enough for that type of business, this example still applies in principle.

I called the first one and asked how much he would charge me for a certain amount of this special paper. "That's expensive paper," he told me. "I can let you have it for $15.00 a ream. (I honestly don't remember the exact price, so I'm just using $15.00 in the example.)

I thanked him, then called the next guy. "I can get this paper for $15.00 a ream, and I need such-and-such an amount of it. Can you do better than that?"

"Well, let me see." Silence while he figured it out. "Yeah. I could let you have it for $10.73 a ream."

"That's wonderful. Thanks very much. I'll call you back later if I want to purchase."

Next guy came down more. The next joined in the bargaining. Before it was over, I brought the price down to something around $5.50 a ream, or about one third of the original asking price. And they still made a good profit, I'm sure.

Ask. Shop. Get to know the persons and places where you can get the best prices for your needs in the music ministry. In the long run, you will save loads of money.

That Will Be $250, Please
What happens at the end of the budget year?

They didn't tell me that at the end of the budget year, when December 31 became January 1, any funds left over in my music budget would be lost. No funds were to be carried over into the future. If you didn't spend it, you lost it.

Not fair, but that's the way it often is. I mean, I was a good boy and didn't overspend the budget. I could really use that money for next year's spring musical. Wouldn't they let me save it and use it then? No way.

Another thing that I didn't think was fair was that if I did overspend one of my categories, they would *subtract* that amount from the following year to make it up. Please give me patience, Lord!

I don't know whether you will face those kinds of rules in your job or not, but I found out from talking with lots of ministers of music that this is a common procedure among churches. Fine. I learned a way around it.

I don't know what you are going to think of this. It's one of those gray areas, perhaps. You decide.

In talking about this situation to the person who was my regular music distributor, he told me that I should do what lots of other ministers of music did. Facing the same challenge, they would tell him in the early weeks of December how much money they had left over in their music budget. He would invoice them for that amount. The church would pay the bill, and he would treat it as credit on the account for future business.

I had $250 left over that December, and I needed it in February for the purchase of an expensive oratorio. So he invoiced me for $250 for the purchase of the oratorio. He just didn't put in the order and deliver the music until I needed it.

Yes, I know. That smacks of dishonesty and manipulation. But it seemed fair to me. I mean, the money was designated for the purchase of music. I wanted to use it in January and February instead of November and December. He allowed me to do that through an accounting entry. It worked.

Misused By Special Permission
The photocopy machine is not intended for breaking copyright laws.

Having just shared with you a little idea that some of you may call bad behavior, I want to conclude this portion by pointing out a practice that I *know* is bad behavior. That's the common exercise of using the handy photocopy machine to reproduce copyrighted music. On this issue, I take a clear stand: Don't do it! It's legally wrong, punishable, and morally unacceptable.

It's a habit. It's a little like potato chips, and it's hard to copy just one. That one was so easy, let's just copy one or two more. Pretty soon, you're addicted.

I distinctly remember one day years ago when my Assistant Minister of Music came into my office with the alarming news that he had just heard about two men from the government who were going through our town. They were making surprise visits to schools and churches, asking to see their music libraries. Obviously they were checking for illegally photocopied music.

The fine, he told me, was something like $10 per page! He knew that we had a few copies in our own library and was wondering what we ought to do about it.

Well, my reply took no thought. "Let's get downstairs to the music library right now, take out the photocopies, and throw them out!"

"All of them?" he asked, rather astonished that I would be willing to give up so much precious music.

"All of them!" I said. "There couldn't be *that* many."

What a surprise I had in store for myself. For years I had made a copy here and a copy there for convenience sake. In most cases it was because I wanted the choir to sing a title that we already owned and had sung before, but now there were not enough copies to go around because the choir had grown so much in size. So we just made a "few" extra copies to allow everyone to have enough music.

By the time we went through the entire library and culled out those glaring examples of criminal offense, I was stunned to discover that we had enough boxes full of the stuff to fill the trunk of my car three times as we drove it to the dumpster!

I'm not proud of that. It was shameful. It's not so surprising that I sinned, but that I sinned so *badly*. We lost a lot of music that day, but we gained a clear conscience. I am so glad that we repented of that practice and that the memory of that shameful day will keep me from a repeat performance.

By the way, those copyright guys never did come by our church to investigate us. But that sort of thing does go on. In fact, The Church Music

Publishers Association has been encouraging individuals to turn in anyone they know who has abused the law in this area. They will prosecute. They should.

If you wish or need to copy music that is protected by copyright laws, ask. It's that simple! Under appropriate circumstances, you will usually receive permission. There may be a slight charge at times, but your conscience will be clear before man and before God.

Yes, the music budget may be too small at times to cover the cost of all the new printed music you want to buy. That does not give you or me the freedom to look the other way and illegally copy music.

Instead, you might set up a system of borrowing music from other churches or organizations that are willing to lend it. But you must be willing to reciprocate.

Best of all, work on getting that music budget up to speed with the real world. It may take several years or more to accomplish, and you may learn more patience than you'd like in the process, but it is definitely the best answer in the long run.

CHAPTER 4

THEY DIDN'T TELL ME

◆ ◆ ◆

I Would Have To Be A Psychologist.

The Situation

D
AN IS A FINE WORSHIP LEADER. He is sensitive to the presence of the Holy Spirit, has a strong love for the Lord, and shows it whenever he is in front of his congregation leading worship.

The choir of his church in Pennsylvania has grown from around 25 participants when Dan came on board to over 75 today — and that happened in less than one year's time.

The congregation is blessed by Dan. The choir is blessed by him. And the Lord is certainly honored by this man's gifts in worship and music.

However, there is one person who is very uncomfortable with what is happening through Dan's anointed leadership — the pastor. It is safe to say that the pastor, whose name is Mark, is threatened.

Have you ever tried to capture an animal that felt threatened? You know the wild reactions you get from it. Well, Mark is acting like a very civilized, very sophisticated, but very threatened animal.

Mark always smiles. He smiles at staff meetings, in the pulpit, in his home visits, driving the car to lunch. One wonders if he smiles in his sleep!

But behind that constant smile is a hurting man. He's in his late 50's. He's had a few health problems. His congregation has been asking questions about his sermons during the past year or so. He just doesn't have the same old spark.

Dan, on the other hand, is going strong. His ministry is holding the church together. Mark knows that. Problem.

Dan went to the staff meeting one week as usual. He stopped by his office just a moment to proofread the Sunday morning bulletin for his secretary. The meeting began at 10:00 a.m.; it was now about 9:59 a.m. When 10:00 a.m. arrived, Dan was still standing by his desk reading. The pastor suddenly appeared at the door. All the secretarial staff was nearby, as were two other staff members preparing to go down the hall to the meeting.

With a voice that shattered the mood of that otherwise tranquil office, Mark said, "Dan, I'm calling you to the staff meeting — NOW! I don't like it when we start late!"

Dan looked up in startled amazement. He looked at his secretary. They both raised their eyebrows, questioning one another without words. What was the pastor's problem today?

That was one of the first signs of trouble. Pastor Mark began to snap at everyone, but his target practice was primarily reserved for Dan. Suddenly nothing Dan planned or recommended was any good. Even some of the worship expressions that the congregation had grown to love were now discontinued.

"I've heard a lot of people complaining," said Mark, "that they don't feel I am the worship leader in this congregation anymore. It's important, Dan, that my people see their pastor as the worship leader. So I want to open the service from now on, and I don't want you to have any part of the prayer time."

No one on the staff could support that. Dan knew in his heart that the pastor was wrong. Yet the pastor was the pastor. So Dan had to comply.

Dan resigned from that position about six months later. By that time, the pastor had succeeded in turning one of the key committees against the worship style that Dan was leading, and things just got too difficult for him to continue.

Part of the problem had to do with church politics. But the root of the problem had to do with the psychology of the situation surrounding a threatened pastor. Dan did not know how to deal with it. Even if he had learned, it might have been too late to change the situation.

***

Joyce is the minister of music of a rather small church in Colorado. She enjoys a full-time position in a town where she is the only full-time minister of music.

Joyce is efficient in everything she does. As a result, she is an over achiever, getting twice as much done as the average person. Her life is beautifully organized by her day-timer calendar. Ask Joyce where she was

I Would Have To Be A Psychologist.

at 8:00 p.m. three months ago today, and she can probably tell you by referring to her notes.

The choir loves Joyce. Her musical leadership is inspired and her ability to organize the music program is almost flawless. The choir always knows two months in advance what anthems they will be singing, so they are usually able to memorize almost all their music.

Joyce started a Worship Team in the church. Their responsibility is to coordinate all the Sunday morning worship services. They get the sermon material and Scripture references from the pastor, then they help choose the hymns, special music, readings, and everything else that goes into making the services cohesive. Their creative input has made a strong impact on the church, and they have helped Joyce tremendously in her task of service coordination. I'm happy to say that Joyce got the details for this idea from my book OPEN THE DOORS.(I just wanted to take the opportunity for a little commercial.)

The pastor is Dr. Fred. This man is an absolute lover. He is a pastor's pastor. If anyone is getting married, baptized, or buried, this is definitely the man they would want. His visits in the hospital are more healing than the physician's. When Dr. Fred prays for you, you really feel prayed for.

His secretary is Mildred, and she's been with him for all of his 23 years as pastor of this little church. Dr. Fred would be lost without Mildred. She keeps his calendar and makes all his appointments. Dr. Fred would never remember his wife's birthday if it were not for Mildred.

In fact, Dr. Fred doesn't even own a calendar. He doesn't need one. He hardly needs a watch, because Mildred is there.

Joyce wants to get the sermon material from Dr. Fred several months in advance so that she and her Worship Team can coordinate the service. Dr. Fred's answer is a warm "I'll try." It never happens. Dr. Fred himself doesn't know what he'll be preaching on until Thursday or Friday of that week. He traditionally outlines the sermon on the day before. Joyce is so frustrated she could scream.

Two different personalities; tons of resulting conflicts and problems.

***

It was my first full-time job as a minister of music. I loved working with the adult choir, and even the teen choir; and I had learned how to make it work pretty well.

Part of my job was to make sure that the children's choir area also went well. No problem: My wife Elizabeth was great with that.

But another part of my job was to direct a junior high group. Since I was so successful with the senior highs, I figured that things should go pretty smoothly here.

Wrong. I'll never forget the day that hurricane of a group stormed into my orderly choir room with their sneakers and bubble gum. By the time I got home for dinner that night, I was so hoarse from yelling that I could hardly talk. Dinner was a daze.

Just as I was recovering from that culture shock, our Minister of Pastoral Care told me that the senior citizens were having a luncheon once a month at the church. He wanted me to come lead some music for them and wondered also if I might be willing to lead a handbell choir just for them.

I didn't know how to say no, so I agreed. I had no idea what I was getting myself into, but inside I felt both benevolent and bewildered.

The music part at the senior citizen luncheons turned out to be sort of fun and easy. As long as I sang "How Great Thou Art" every month and also talked about my two little children, they were very happy indeed.

Then the handbell choir group met. Lovely ladies, every one of them. Gentle spirits, and so appreciative. But could they count? Are you kidding? Could they ever be a handbell choir? Well, sort of. It was a real challenge. And they wanted to play in church as soon as possible! Oh my. Should I or shouldn't I?

While pondering that question, I got a visit from a sweet gal by the name of Vicki who told me that she wanted to get involved in our music program by starting a preschool children's choir. Could I help her?

Preschool? Sounded like a great idea to me, but what did I know about that? Absolutely nothing. I didn't study music education in college. I didn't have field experience with preschool, junior high, or senior citizens. In fact, I considered it a minor miracle that I was doing so well with the high school bunch.

They didn't tell me that when I became a minister of music, I would have to be an expert in the psychology of all age groups — from four to ninety-four. Help!

I Would Have To Be A Psychologist.

* * *

Ruth was a strong lady. Her husband Tom was a strong and proud man. They were both very active in the church. Ruth sang in the choir; Tom served on the Administrative Committee.

Great people. Loved the Lord and served Him in many ways. But I didn't get along very well with either one of them.

You see, I did and said some things in choir rehearsal one night that I thought were cute and funny. Ruth was offended. She went home and told Tom. He was offended. I was totally unaware of their feelings.

Then it came time for my job review. Tom was not only on the Administrative Committee, he was Chairman of the committee. That's when I came face to face with what felt like a meat cleaver.

Pain. Conflict. It all ended up with that couple and I meeting together with Gary, one of the pastors on our staff. We sat together and communicated. Gary was the mediator. It was resolved, thank God, and life moved on.

But then one of the other staff members of the church and I began to lock horns. The worst part was that he happened to be the senior pastor. He wanted me to do something that I just did not want to do. I said so. He was crushed. I believe, in his mind, he thought I was unspiritual about my stand. In my mind, I was just being honest.

So there was another meeting. Gary came again as the mediator. It was good but not fun. And it was only one of a number of similar meetings in the future.

Then there was the time when one of my other staff colleagues really dropped the ball. He and I were jointly responsible for a big project that involved some major money and lots of people. He didn't do his part, but he told me that he had. Not only did he let me and lots of other people down, but he simply lied to me about it.

When the moment of truth came, and I discovered his failure and his cover-up, I was so angry that I couldn't even talk about it. I had to leave the building, drive around in the car, and just collect my thoughts.

Gary hosted another good meeting between us. Thank God for Gary! He was a psychologist in his training, and he introduced me to the term "conflict management."

In fact, Gary used to joke that I was keeping him in business. "You just keep creating the conflicts, Harry, and I'll come along and manage them. We make a great team!"

They didn't tell me that I would need to learn to manage conflicts. In the church? You mean to tell me that people have conflicts in God's house? You bet.

I Would Have To Be A Psychologist.

The biggest problem with any church is that it is infested with people. People have conflicts; and in a loving church environment, those conflicts need to be resolved.

Gary taught me some extremely valuable lessons in that area. God used those conflicts to help equip me.

Jason has been a minister of music for a long, long time. I asked him what had been the greatest challenge of his career — not a specific challenge, but a general one.

"That's easy," he responded. "The biggest challenge for me has been to find ways to motivate my people."

Nobody told me that I would have to be a motivator.

I thought all the people who like to sing and who have ever sung would want to join the choir.

I thought all the people who joined the choir would be eager to attend rehearsals and be on time.

I thought all the choir people would love all the different styles of music I love.

I thought asking the choir to memorize the music would cause them to flock to the task like sea gulls flocking to a school of fish.

I thought teen-agers would enjoy singing and would want to be in a choir.

I thought the lovely sound of handbells would cause me to have to turn people away when I started that group.

I thought going on a full weekend retreat with the choir would be everyone's idea of the perfect way to spend their weekend.

It doesn't matter what I thought, Jason had a good point. People in America are often stressed out. They live and work in the fast lane. When they have an opportunity to relax, they want to take it. Asking them to do more in the church music program is not always that easy.

Besides that, there are many different types of personalities in this world. What one person loves, another might detest. As one person so aptly put it, "Different strokes for different folks."

You have to learn how to motivate people — all types of people — if you're going to succeed in the music ministry.

Choir rehearsal was just finished, and we were all getting our coats and saying our goodbyes. Cindy was so short that I almost didn't see her standing right in front of me as I was getting ready to leave the choir room.

"Harry, could I talk to you just a minute?"

"Sure, Cindy, what's up?"

"I need to talk to somebody, and something you said tonight in rehearsal made me feel that perhaps you're the person."

"Well, I'll be glad to listen. What's the problem? You seem really up tight."

"Harry, my husband and I are having some real problems. Our marriage is, our marriage is… well, it's falling apart."

"Cindy, I had no idea. I'm so sorry."

"Thank you. But I've just got to get some help. I'm a nervous wreck."

At that point, the tears began to come. Not in trickles, but in buckets. I began to realize that this dear lady was entrusting to me some very personal and heavy problems. She was looking to me for some type of support or advice. Then the kickers came.

"Harry, I've not shared this with anyone else, OK? But I trust you with this. My husband beats me. On several occasions, I've had to go for medical help. And now I suspect that he's molesting our little daughter."

Sobs followed. She practically fell into my arms with grief. I was both shocked at what she was telling me and desperately searching for words to say to her that I thought would show wisdom. Then she suddenly got very sober, no tears, and looked me squarely in the eye.

"What would the Lord have me do in a situation like this?"

There I was, on the spot. She wanted me to be not only her confidant, but her counselor as well.

They didn't tell me I would be asked to be a counselor.

Cindy and I worked through her problems for many weeks and months. She went through some rough times, but her life is in order now.

There was nothing in the school of music curriculum that prepared me for her questions. How was I supposed to know that my choir members would begin to see me as a spiritual leader with counseling abilities?

Cindy is just one example of countless others. In fact, there were times that I wondered if someone had placed a sign outside my office without my knowledge reading "The Counselor Is In."

Of all the folks who wanted to turn to me for advice and help, none was more evident than the teen-agers. Boys with sex problems, girls with

I Would Have To Be A Psychologist.

boy problems, boys and girls with parent problems, career decisions, love lives that rivaled soap operas. They would consume me at times, and I found it difficult not to take on their problems as if they were my own.

I often found myself meeting with the parents and some of those teens. There were times when I had to go to their homes and stick my nose in, if you will.

I mentioned in the discussion about being married to the job that the telephone rang at home all the time. Many of those calls were for counseling. In fact, all those calls that came at 2:00 a.m. were counseling-related. It just seems that there are many needy people in churches. Not materially poor, necessarily, but spiritually and emotionally impoverished. They are hungry for authentic love and help. As one of their spiritual leaders, they will turn to you.

1981 was perhaps the worst year of my life. During that year lots of different things seemed to fall in on me.

My wife and I experienced three deaths in our family — two parents and a baby.

I changed jobs, and I was not happy in the move. We missed our old friends so much that we became homesick.

Elizabeth and I both had to have surgery during that year. Recovery for each of us was not easy.

I decided that I was going to leave the job I was in and take the risk of being a free-lance minister of music. Elizabeth was not working at the time, we had no savings, and we owed a huge sum of money to the church I was leaving (they had given us a generous loan to help with our housing costs).

That's the overview. Believe me, I was feeling sorry for myself.

Those were all stress-producing situations. Stress is an interesting thing. It can sneak up on you. God can seem very far away. You lose weight that you would rather keep. Your immune system is weakened so that you are more likely to get sore throats, flu, or worse, depression sets in so that your attitude is like a flat tire. You know — all the "fun" things of life.

Don't forget — you are one of the church's spiritual leaders. Others have you on some type of pedestal where Gos is in His heaven and all is well in your world. Sunday after Sunday you are expected to stand before the hungry crowd and feed them their spiritual nourishment for the week. Lead them into the inner court with the Father — a place you can't seem to find for yourself, much less for them.

All that can produce even more stress in one's life. It's a vicious cycle.

You always thought working in the church would be easy? Guess again. You will probably have times when you will not only have to learn to deal with other people's stress, but your own as well.

*
* *

Choir members are an interesting species. They are followed closely by church secretaries as one of the most intriguing specimens of human life.

Those who love to sing in the church choir are usually people with artistic natures. They love music (we certainly hope they do, anyway), and they are likely to be those folks who love to write poetry, draw, listen to symphonies, compose, perform, and do needlepoint.

Some like it hot, some like it cold. Like the pastor, the committee members, and all the rest of the people in the pews, those in your choir will have a variety of personalities. And they won't all be like yours.

Shocked? Of course not. But knowing this tidbit and living with it are two entirely different ball games.

If you are going to be the leader of personalities, you need to know something about them. Not only that, you need to know something about your *own* personality. What are you like? How do others perceive you?

Yes, indeed, to be a well-rounded minister of music, you need to be an amateur psychologist.

I Would Have To Be A Psychologist.

Some Solutions

And Now, Heeerrrrs Johnny!
Life is full of interesting personalities for you to deal with.

IN EVERY CHOIR, ON EVERY CHURCH STAFF, in every congregation, you are going to encounter a large variety of personality types. You yourself fall into one of the many categories.

Sometimes opposites attract, but at other times they are the things that peace treaties are all about.

What are some of the typical types you will encounter in the choir? Learning to recognize them is the first step in learning how to deal with them. Here's a partial list that all choir directors will recognize.

The Clinger

This is the person who will love you — forever. They just want to walk in your shadow. Before rehearsal they will come up to you just to ask how you are, is there anything they can do for you, how is your family, guess what I heard the other day — anything they can think of to have a conversation with you.

They often love to touch you. You will know who it is immediately when they come up behind you and surprisingly put their hands on your shoulders as if to give you a back rub. Or perhaps their favorite greeting will be to give you a great big hug from the rear, followed by a sweet, "Guess who!"

These and all other personality types come in both male and female varieties, but women seem to be more prone to this behavior. They love being seen with you, so you can be sure that they will hang around at the end of rehearsal to make sure you get to your car all right.

You'll like your clinger: They are good for your ego. But you'll often wish they wouldn't invade your space so much.

I Would Have To Be A Psychologist.

The Complainer

This is the one person who is never satisified. They are happiest when they are miserable. And they want everyone else to be the same.

You can count on their not liking your choice of music. The whole choir will know that they don't like it, either by the pointed questions they will make in front of everyone, or by the way they make unmistakable comments supposedly intended only for the person sitting next to them.

Notice their facial expression when you announce the fall retreat or the extra rehearsals for the Christmas music. And if you ever need to bring up anything that concerns money, watch out!

Don't think you have things under control if the Complainer isn't making waves at rehearsal. Most of their work is done behind the scenes, especially on the telephone.

The Director

"The sopranos aren't getting those notes."

"Don't you think that's a little too fast?"

"Could you give us a better cut off right there? I can't tell what you want us to do."

Usually this choir member will enjoy telling you how much they enjoy singing in choirs, especially since the time they sang under Dr. Super Music in college. Sometimes they will also have a music degree, having studied for four years in order to teach public school music.

They are knowledgeable. The problem is they want you and everybody else to know it.

I Would Have To Be A Psychologist.

The Judge

This is a person who would be happier in a court room than in a choir room. They have an opinion on everything, and it is always in black or white.

You won't have to ask them what their opinion is: Just ask the three or four persons sitting around them in the choir rehearsal. They will all have heard the words of wisdom spewing forth between each rest in the music.

Their opinions are not always wrong, and that's one of the things that makes them an annoying asset to your organization. You will need their opinions, and it will be very helpful whenever their opinion agrees with your own.

If you said that rehearsal would be over by 9:00 p.m., then you'd better not go until 9:05. If you do, Big Ben would be a soft chime in comparison to the reaction you'll hear.

By the way, they probably won't think your jokes are very funny.

THEY DIDN'T TELL ME...

The Turtle

No matter what you try to do with this person, you will never speed them up. Not only are they always the slowest one to understand your instructions, get their robe on, organize their music, and all the rest, but they are always, always late. In fact, they will be the running joke in the choir because of their lack of punctuality. The Judge will glare at The Turtle, and you'll be expected to DO SOMETHING ABOUT IT!

By the way, if you expect every choir member to have a pencil in his or her folder, you'd better have a few spares on hand: The Turtle won't be able to find theirs.

I Would Have To Be A Psychologist.

The Prima Donna

It is a rare Prima Donna who is not a soprano. I don't know why this is so, but that section of the choir just seems more vulnerable to this malady.

The Prima Donna needs a little extra attention. Make that *tons* of extra attention. They need affirmation and lots of opportunities to be "on stage."

The person who probably suffers the most with the Prima Donna is the accompanist. The poor accompanist can probably play better than the Prima Donna can sing, but the Prima Donna loves to tell the accompanist just how the piece must be done.

Not all Prima Donnas are unpleasant personalities: Many of them are rather sweet. But they do have a fat case of vanity.

The Florist

Life is so sweet for the Florist. Coming to choir rehearsal is like slowly sinking into a tub of warm water bubbles — AAAhhhhhhhh.

Whenever you look at them, their eyes light up with glee. They love for you to notice them.

Watch out: The Florist is a die-hard romanticist. In fact, they fall in love with love. If you're not careful, they will also fall in love with you!

I Would Have To Be A Psychologist.

The Witness

Regardless of how hard you try to motivate people to get involved, some just sit back and watch everybody else do the work. For the Witness, life moves on and moves by. They don't participate.

You won't have to deal with most of the folks who fit this category, except in hearing them give you one of the many reasons why they just can't sing in the choir.

There must be an underground newspaper published for The Witness giving them the most often used reasons for not participating. Number one on the list seems to be "I'm too busy." Funny — all those folks who do use their God-given talents to worship Him must not have anything else to do.

The second most frequent excuse from that underground publication is "I'm too tired." Unique group of people, these Witnesses: They are the only busy, tired people in the church on Wednesday and Thursday nights while those countless others who have idle time on their hands and abundant energy to burn just have to go to choir rehearsal to take care of that problem.

The Soap Opera Star

This is a very sad person. All of life's crises seem to follow him or her, no matter what.

Their life is really too complicated for them to be in the choir in the first place. They need to be home, in counseling, or possibly in therapy.

You will hear all the plots and subplots of their intriguing life. You will probably earn your Master's Degree in counseling through the time you devote to their woes.

One of the best things about having this Star on your team is that you will learn better how to pray.

*
**

I Would Have To Be A Psychologist.

These are just some of those interesting personalities God allows us to encounter along the way. They are what one author once called "Grace Builders" — the more you deal with them, the more grace you need to sustain your own life.

Can you learn to understand and deal with these multiple personalities? Yes. At least you can get a good start. One of the most beneficial exercises I have experienced in this area is the Myers-Briggs Type Indicator exam. With this simple written test, a person's basic personality characteristics can be analyzed. His or her preferences in life are revealed, and great understanding for one another emerges.

Not only does this test give you a profile of the personality and preferences of your fellow staff members, but it gives you a valuable picture of yourself as well.

Sitting together and discussing the results of this little survey is extremely enlightening. Within a matter of minutes things begin to make more sense. Is *that* why he acts that way? Is *that* why she's so irritated with me when I do that?

You ought to know about this test, take it yourself, and consider having every member of your choir take it as well. The process can be really fun, and people ought to be able to relate to one another with much more charity as a result.

Knowing where you are weak and they are strong creates a sense of understanding between people. Also, Christians can better celebrate the variety of gifts that God gives to us. Instead of criticizing the pastor for his weaknesses (when he's different from me), I can rejoice over his strengths (areas of my weakness where I need him to complement me). What a difference that makes!

Here are some of the basic revelations that the Myers-Briggs test offers:

1. We all need to understand that how we perceive things is not always the way others perceive them. That has much to do with what we call our "belief system." I believe I am fat, so I won't wear a bathing suit. I believe that I can't sing well, so I just won't sing. I believe that I'm not smart enough to do that, so I won't try.

2. People take in information and act on it in different ways. Some of us receive information primarily by our senses — with our eyes and ears. Others take in information primarily

by intuition. We use both of course; but most people are stronger in one area than the other. Those who prefer to use the senses to take in facts are often more realistic. Those who are more intuitive place a higher value on imagination and inspiration, thus often becoming more visionary.

3. When it comes to deciding things, some of us are "thinkers," while others are "feelers." Thinkers are often more logical in their approach than the feelers are, and that can certainly cause conflicts. The thinkers among us love to analyze objectively; the feelers tend to be more sympathetic and tactful.

4. When people of different personality types approach a situation, they usually see it from opposite points of view. They probably don't understand or even think of the point of view that the other person has. If they can learn to appreciate this phenomenon, then they can be mutually helpful to one another in problem solving.

5. When two persons of extremely opposite personality types have to work together (as is often true of pastor and church musician), a full understandng of these matters can do a tremendous amount of good in lessening the inevitable friction between them.

6. We tend to be either extroverted or introverted in our approach to the world around us. All of us are a combination of the two, but each of us has a preference. Some are more comfortable working actively with other people or with things; others would prefer to work alone and with ideas instead.

So we are all different. We perceive things differently, we take in information differently, we solve problems differently. God designed each of us that way and pronounced it good. Though our preferences in life situations vary, we must learn to recognize these differences and mutually respect one another.

Perhaps as a musician you would like to think of different personality types using terms more common to your vocabulary. How about these:

Expressivo: The feeling person, possibly your Prima Donna

Adagio: This is your Turtle who is always late

Bravura: Usually in the bass section, and definitely irritable

Sforzando: A trouble maker who is full of surprises

Marcato: This person loves to be in control

Dolce: Your most lovable singer — one we wish we had more of

Spirito: One who is full of spirit, but not always the holy kind

Those are fun, but there is a lot of truth there. And then there's me, myself, and I. What categories do I fall into? How do the choir members perceive me? Do I like what they perceive, or would I like for them to get to know the "real me?"

Fascinating thoughts. Life-changing questions. Let me highly recommend that you become more knowledgeable about personality preferences, possibly through the Myer-Briggs Type Indicator exam. You may write to the publishers for more information:

> Consulting Psychologists Press, Inc.
> 577 College Avenue
> Palo Alto, CA 94306

In addition to this resource, I suggest that you go to your local library and check out some books on this subject. If you have any opportunities to go to workshops dealing with this area — ones designed for the layman — then do it. Your music ministry may be more helped by your becoming more knowledgeable in the area of human psychology than by your learning yet another set of new releases from the music publishers.

Stop, Look, and Listen
Learning and teaching listening skills can revolutionize your ministry.

I never knew that I needed to learn how to listen. I mean, I was born able to hear, wasn't I?

In graduate school my minor was in counseling. It was there that I began to learn that there is an art, a skill to listening carefully and effectively.

People with problems will come to you. What they most want is for someone to listen. You may not ever be equipped to professionally and successfully handle all the problems that will cross your path through those marvelous and incredible folks in your choir, but you must and you can learn to *listen*.

Here are some of the things you need to do to develop good listening skills:

1. Keep your eyes on the one you are hearing. Wandering eyes are a sure sign that you are not in touch with what they are saying.

2. Keep your hands still. Fighting with a hangnail or drumming your fingers on the table are big no-no's.

3. Listen for the overall message coming to you. If you concentrate too much on details, you may miss the point altogether.

4. Decide up front that this person is worth listening to, regardless of your physical, mental, or emotional state at the moment. Remember that the Bible tells us that we sometimes entertain angels unaware. Maybe this person is one of God's little tests for you.

5. Concentrate. Be sincere. It's easy to pretend you are listening when your mind is actually outlining your rehearsal plans.

6. Let them talk. They want you to listen, not necessarily give them answers. I'll say more about that below.

7. Divorce your emotions if necessary. Sometimes we can get emotionally hooked into what we are hearing and thereby lose good judgment.

8. Communicate through your face, your eyes, your posture, and your verbal responses that you are interested in what they are saying. A person often doesn't get to the real meat of their problem until they test the waters with you a little. You'll have to win them over before you can be of real help in hearing them.

One of the terms that's been used considerably is "Active Listening." That's a great and descriptive term, implying that you are really doing something in the process — you are not passive.

I Would Have To Be A Psychologist.

One of my friends jokes about one of his problems. He is gifted at active interrupting! That's a big problem in the listening/counseling department. Don't interrupt them while they are pouring out their heart.

When you do get a chance to speak, tell them this: "I hear you saying that..." or "What I hear you saying is..." What follows is your sincere effort to feed back to them the words and the feelings that they are communicating to you. It encourages them to know that you are really hearing them, and it helps them continue to get it all out.

Ask questions. The questions you ask, however, are not necessarily for you to be able to gain more information: They are intended to help the other person identify their own feelings. You may ask the questions in the same way that you mirror what they are saying to you. For instance, "Is it fair to say that you were deeply hurt by what she did?"

"Yes, yes, I was. That's right. She hurt me deeply." Then you are bound to hear more about that hurt.

Stay on their subject. If they want to talk about their teen-ager's drinking problem, don't ask them to describe their husband's temper problem. Not yet, anyway.

Show them that you empathize with what they are saying, but don't fall into the most common trap of all. Many, many amateur counselors empathize by saying, "I can really identify with you. I had a very similar problem with my mother." Then they are off and running with their example. The here's-how-I-handled-the-problem monologue is probably the last thing the person needs or wants to hear from you, so keep it to yourself. Right now they feel like they are the only person in the world with this problem, and they need to talk about it.

Later, after the initial conversation, you may indeed wish to reveal to the person your own experiences with a similar situation. That will help them realize how well you understood what they were saying, and they will hopefully be able to understand that their problem is not as unique as it may have felt in the first place.

Listening is indeed an art. Some people seem to have a natural ability to do it well, but most of us need to practice it. Just like you would practice the organ before the Sunday service, you need to practice good listening habits.

If you can get some professional or semiprofessional training in this area, wonderful. Take it. Get others to take it with you.

If that's difficult to do, then take the tips above and start applying them today to anybody and everybody. Believe me, it works. But unless you practice, you won't grow in this area.

You might share these ideas with someone else — such as a staff colleague or your spouse. Monitor one another when you are in listening situations together. How well did I do? Did I give advice that wasn't being asked for? Did I interrupt? What did you hear him say? Does it coincide with what I heard?

You can be assured that your listening skills will be severely tested. The most common way is for someone to approach you at the wrong time in the wrong way. They will probably be angry. It will flash in their eyes and blaze through their throat. One of the favorite times for this to happen is just before the Sunday service is to begin, and it might even be the pastor who is the culprit.

What do you do? Stay calm. The problem does not have to be solved that very moment. Don't become defensive — your natural inclination. Try not to answer anger with anger. Listen, listen, listen. Let them get it out.

No, it's not fun; but it's absolutely necessary that they do get it out — all over you. No, you probably don't deserve it; but that's not the issue at the moment. This person is fiery mad — that's the issue.

If the moment they've chosen is an impossible one, tell them, "I really want to hear this. It's important. But obviously I have to be in the choir loft in about five minutes. Could you please meet me right after the service so that we can set a mutually convenient time to continue this. I'll make myself available to you." They will probably realize the instant you speak those words that they've just made a big goof. They will be embarrassed. Let them be. Then follow through with that meeting.

One of the best gifts you can give to your choir is to raise up shepherds among them. These are people who will be an extension of you in the pastoring areas that are common in every choir. But each of those shepherds should be trained to listen. They will probably be your ears in the group, anyway. If they can learn the basics of good active listening along with you, their effectiveness will be easily multiplied by ten.

Managing conflicts in your own life and in the lives of those with whom you minister depends on your ability to listen. You will have many times when conflict management will be the order of the day, so hear me well. Do yourself a favor: Open your ears. Help others to hear one another. That's communication. Without it, you will never survive the job.

First You Must Go
The "Matthew Principle" saves both time and relationships.

Jesus was the greatest psychologist of all, and He taught us a cardinal principle of conflict management in two places in the book of Matthew. You should master it. Then you should make sure that everyone with whom you work on the church staff masters it. Share it with all your committee members as well, and then teach it with fervor to all your choir members.

The two passages are in Matthew 5 and Matthew 18.

Matthew 5:23-24

> Therefore, if you are offering your gift at the altar and there remember that your brother has something

against you, leave your gift there in front of the altar. First go and be reconciled to your brother; then come and offer your gift.

Matthew 18:15-17

If your brother sins against you, go and show him his fault, just between the two of you. If he listens to you, you have won your brother over.

But if he will not listen, take one or two others along, so that every matter may be established by the testimony of two or three witnesses.

If he refuses to listen to them, tell it to the church; and if he refuses to listen even to the church, treat him as you would a pagan or a tax collector.

Now notice something about these two passages. They have one very vital thing in common. The word is "Go." In the first passage, you have sinned against someone else; in the second passage, someone has sinned against you. But in both passages, *you* are to *go*.

Jesus didn't say if you have sinned, or if they have sinned against you, pray about it. And He most definitely didn't say talk to other people about it. That's the common reaction of most people when they are mad at someone else: They talk about it to everyone except the one with whom they need to reconcile.

People in your choir are going to get upset with you. I know, you are one of the most lovable people on the planet Earth. You have a mother. All dogs like you. Besides that, you are a committed Christian and all your sins are covered by the blood of Christ. Nevertheless, you are going to cause someone to have elevated blood pressure.

At that point in time, you need to go to them. But if you don't realize you've done anything wrong, then they need to come to you — according to the teachings in Matthew.

You will need to remind your choir members and co-workers of this principle repeatedly. Someone will have to remind you about it as well. And you need to let people know that you *want* them to come to you. Let them know that the gate is open. Reveal the awful truth — you are human! Cultivate this kind of relationship among your choir members and see the result.

There is a wonderful passage in II Chronicles 5 in which Solomon was dedicating his glorious temple. We learn that the priests were there, the elders, the ark of the covenant, and the king himself. They sacrificed so many animals that day that the number could not even be recorded.

They had a great time of "playing church." But then something very wonderful happened — the glory of the Lord filled the temple. God revealed some of Himself to those worshipers. Thrilling!

And do you know when and how that happened? It was when the song of the choir was raised, accompanied by 120 trumpets! I love that! God responded to the music!

But what was so special about that music? What was it that pleased God so much as to cause Him to fill that temple with His glory? Was it because the choir sang in tune? Was it because there was no taped accompaniment? Or perhaps it was because there were enough tenors for a change.

No. The answer is found in verse 13 of that chapter: "The trumpeters and singers joined in unison, as with one voice, to give praise and thanks to the Lord." The word "unison" there is the same root as the word "unity." That was one moment in time when God's appointed church musicians were of one mind, one heart, one spirit, one voice.

That's the calling for all church musicians today, too. But that will only happen when they learn to do what Jesus said to do in Matthew. That will only happen when you, their shepherd under the Lord, lead them to practice those important principles of reconciliation in love.

Stop the World: I Wanna Get Off
You need to learn how to handle your own personal stress.

What good are you in the ministry if you are stressed out? How positive can you be in front of your choir when everything you are thinking is negative?

Stress will come. Sometimes it will be minor and short-lived; but if the other type pays you a visit, you need to deal with it. You need to manage your own stress so that you will be whole enough to help others manage theirs.

Here are some rambling thoughts. Since they are thoughts, please think about them.

1. When you discover you are under stress, admit it to yourself. Find someone to whom you can talk. The worst thing you can do is keep it in. That's not spiritual. That's not strong. That's dumb.

2. Stress lowers your body's immune system. Take some vitamin and mineral supplements with your diet, and make sure you eat properly. That may mean changing some of your eating habits, but do it.

3. You are going to need extra rest. I didn't say sleep, because you may feel like you'll never get enough of that. You may find that you are not sleeping well at all. But rest is something you can do even when you're awake. Schedule rest.

4. Look for some recreation in your life. If you have to treat that the same way you would treat going shopping for clothes, then go shopping for recreation. If possible, make it a vacation. Really get away. If you don't have the money for that, ask the church to help you. Don't be too proud to ask.

5. Surround yourself with positive people. The last thing you need right now is to get into regular conversations with those who just join in with your complaints.
6. Laugh. If that means going to the movies to see a comedy, go. Or read a funny book. Take the children to the zoo and laugh at the monkeys. Tickle yourself with a feather. Whatever it takes, laugh.

Remember that managing your own stress will take some time. If it took you a long time to get into this situation, then allow a long time to recover.

If you are married, the normal tendency will be to bring home all your woes. Having a spouse to talk to about problems is one of the greatest benefits of marriage; but if you're not careful, you will turn that poor spouse into a basket case. You may need to protect that person from some or all of the stress-producing garbage you can, but you will certainly want them to know what is going on in your life. Don't withdraw from them: That would be as bad as dumping all your problems on them and then rolling over to go to sleep.

Above all, remember that God never slumbers and never sleeps. His loving care for you is always there, even when you don't feel it. Thank Him for His steadfastness. Admit to Him when you feel the loss of joy from your own salvation. Ask Him to help you through the whole scene. He will. It may seem like He's taking His good sweet time, but He has it all under control.

From Da Capo to Fine
Hiring and firing personnel needs to be handled very carefully.

Whether you are bringing someone on board with you for the first time, or whether you are having to send that person off to read the classified ads, you need to have some principles clearly in mind.

One of them is that you should not perform either of these duties flying solo. You may have to do much of the work alone, but you need the combined wisdom and the protection of other people around you.

Here is one place where a committee is a good thing. That may be a committee of two — you and the senior pastor — but I would recommend to both of you that some of the laymen in your church need to be part of the process, too. It doesn't matter to me whether you are hiring the senior associate pastor or the janitor, do it in concert with other brothers and sisters.

Check references. You may think this person is definitely an angel in disguise. You may be convinced beyond convincing that he or she can do the job with gusto. Doesn't matter: Check the references.

You see, the most competent, the most experienced, the best looking applicant you are able to attract to your establishment needs to have a spiritual commitment to the Lordship of Jesus Christ, needs to know how to work well under authority, needs to have some skills in working well with people, and needs to be morally upright.

Everybody sins. Everybody makes mistakes. You aren't looking for a perfect person, are you? Of course not. But there may be a problem in one or more of these categories that will cause you lots of time in counseling later, no small amount of embarrassment, and possibly the dreaded time of giving that person their departing speech. Check them out.

Don't go by all those nice letters of reference they bring in for you to see. You can believe those letters, but you also need to pick up the telephone and call some of those people. Ask direct questions. You are about to make a very important decision that affects that person's future, your future, and the future of the congregation whom you serve. Ask very direct questions to those who say they are willing to recommend.

All that will help you avoid surprises. Don't let it bother you too much if you do uncover some disappointing news. People change. People mature and repent. Just make sure that if the disappointment is in a critical area, your applicant has indeed changed.

Be honest with the applicant. Let them know if you have a question or concern. Give them every opportunity to explain their side of the story. Know that you will be beginning your work together with openness.

What about you? Are you tough to work with? Do you have some pet peeves? What brings out the worst in you? They deserve to know that before you have them sign the dotted line. So if they aren't smart or experienced enough to ask you those tough questions, tell them anyway.

And the "dotted line" is important. Have a clearly written, thorough job description drawn up for that person to read and sign *before* you hire them. I'm amazed at how many persons get into a job thinking they know what the job is all about, only to discover after they make the commitment that there are some surprises.

I guess the summary of all that I'm saying here is that there should be no surprises — on either side.

By the way, are you willing to yield to the collective wisdom of a search committee? You need to be. You may think that you know just who ought to be hired, but a committee might disagree. God has a way of protecting us when we have blind spots. One of the ways He does that is by the counsel of many.

Now what about the other end of this relationship? If that day comes when you feel that you have to let someone go, it is again crucial that you do so in concert with others. And the senior pastor is *not* sufficient.

I've heard many stories from ministers of music who have had to fire an organist for one reason or another. Most often the reasons are for sexual sins, sad to say. The minister of music and the pastor confer. They counsel with the offender. They concur that there is only one alternative, and the worst must be done.

So they act on it. The minister of music has to tell the choir that a change was made. The pastor may even come to the choir rehearsal and give support to the fact that the decision was a mutual one and done as lovingly as possible.

The next thing that will happen — I guarantee it — is that some of the avid supporters of that poor "victim" you just kicked out into the streets will start a crucifixion against you and the pastor. It never fails. I've known some very fine ministers of music who have made this fatal error. They assume that if the pastor knows all about it and agrees, their bases are all covered. They're not.

Obviously you want to protect that poor soul from public scrutiny. Obviously you want to see to it that the process doesn't end up as a spectacle. But you and the senior pastor need the covering of others in the church who concur with you that there is no other alternative. You need a select committee and/or the rest of the church staff. You need to set up a process that will allow adequate time to go by so that you can be sure there is no possiblity of restoration of that person before the Lord and/or your church. That, after all, should be a higher priority than just getting rid of the problem.

Are you strong enough to allow a person to confess their sin and repent? Truly repent? That takes more time and more effort than firing.

That takes a mature Christian person. It's not always the convenient way around the barn, but it honors the Lord more.

Now if you do have to go through with it, be gentle. If anger is involved, get that healed before you have to continue. If you need to confess anything to that person, do so. If you have to forgive lots of things, do so. Make sure that they leave under the best of circumstances — hugging, if possible. Then stand by them as much as you can.

Perhaps Your Goose Is Cooked
A threatened pastor is a sure ticket to job hunting.

There is a common malady among some pastors — They have a "Messiah Complex". Don't get too excited. That doesn't make them any worse than you and your perpetual ego trip! But pastors, God love 'em, tend to be on that same ego journey. It's just that they tend to feel more spiritual about their condition than they do about yours.

One of the worst things that can happen to you and your pension plan is for you to do such a good job that the pastor is threatened. If that happens, watch out.

How do you avoid that? Well, certainly not by doing a *bad* job! You may not be able to avoid it, as a matter of fact. But if it happens to you, recognize it and try your best to deal with it. Your goose may be cooked, and you may have to move on. But there are a few proactive things you can apply.

First of all, when you place yourself under the spiritual authority of a pastor, really mean it. Tell him so. That's more humbling to him than it is to you. And that's really where you ought to be anyway — under his authority.

Then pray for him. Pray for all of those in authority. Submitting to authority that's not prayed for takes a lot of courage.

Remember the story I shared about the associate pastor who came into the senior pastor's office and said he was there to serve him, to wash his feet? That's the best attitude you can have. Do that. Such humility you haven't seen in your life since mommy had to change your diapers, but you can handle it.

Find out what his priorities are. Does he believe that prayer is the most important thing for his church right now? Then let him know you

I Would Have To Be A Psychologist.

understand that. Let him know that you hear him and you will join with him in communicating that concern to the choir and to the whole church through your own ministry.

People need to be stroked. You need it; your pastor needs it. So when he does something well, be sure to tell him so. Did you really like last Sunday's sermon? Then write him a note and let him know how much it ministered to you. He'll love hearing that kind of compliment in front of the whole staff, too. Human nature is human nature.

I'm certainly not advocating that you be dishonest with yourself or with him. I am trying to say, instead, that you may need to take extra steps to make extra sure that your pastor is extra secure. You can make him or break him with your attitude and your actions. If your working relationship with him is never going to work out, at least you will leave the situation with a good conscience. Hopefully, it will help you get a good recommendation from him as well.

Remember Proverbs 21:1? It says, "The king's heart is in the hand of the Lord; he directs it like a watercourse wherever he pleases." That simply means that your pastor's heart is in God's hands. So if you have trouble with your pastor, go above his head!

CHAPTER 5

THEY DIDN'T TELL ME

◆ ◆ ◆

I Would Have To Be A Producer.

The Situation

I**INHERITED A VERY SPECIAL TEEN CHOIR** when I took my first full-time music ministry job. They were called The Young Folk. They had been together for only one year when I came on board, and they had only sung two or three times for small affairs. But they were really on fire for the Lord!

You see, a number of the kids had gone to a great Young Life summer camp together. There they met the Lord and became totally committed to Him in the refreshing way that only young people can.

As they returned home to Cincinnati that summer, they asked one another how they could share this enthusiasm with the congregation and with the other senior high kids who didn't go along. How could they keep their own spirits high as well?

The conclusion they reached was that they would share the music they had learned at this really neat camp with anybody who would listen. We are talking about the late 60's. That music was Christian folk music with guitar accompaniment.

I was fresh out of graduate school. If I was going to get into this church music thing with both feet, I had decided that I was going to keep my standards high. When I heard that these kids wanted me to lead their group through guitar-accompanied folk music, I elevated my nose high above their level of non-sophistication and said "NO!"

But they prayed for me. The church was patient with me. Those kids asked me if I would at least come to the home of one of the members where they were practicing on a Thursday night and hear them. I really didn't want to do it, but I said yes. I thought to myself that I needed to get this over with as quickly as possible. I was prepared to give them a speech about how busy I was and how I really knew nothing about their style of music. I didn't even play guitar!

So we met. What a wonderful night it was! Those young people showed a love for Jesus Christ and love for one another that I had never seen before. I knew that I was in the presence of authentic Christianity.

Make no mistake about it: People are hungry for the Lord. If what you are offering in your music ministry is authentic, people will flock to it. If what you are offering is just a music program, no big shakes.

Well, those teen-agers had me hooked. Fighting back tears, I honestly told them about the speech I had prepared to give them that night. But then I added how touched I was by their enthusiasm and commitment. So if they would be patient with me while I learned about their style of music, I would try to work with them. At least I was sure I could improve their sound and help them stay together more.

That was the beginning of an incredible ten years together. The original group of about a dozen kids grew into an auditioned group of 60. We made three record albums together, sang on television, sang in countless churches all over Cincinnati on Sunday nights, and toured the United States for two weeks each summer on a Greyhound bus (they didn't tell me I would have to organize choir tours). My life was deeply touched by theirs, and I can say the ministry that the Lord led me to offer those young people changed their lives as well.

But boy, was I ever like a fish out of water at the beginning of this thing. I had a lot to learn.

One thing I knew from the start just by listening, those kids and their style of gentle music needed sound reinforcement. I knew nothing about microphones, nothing about amplifiers, nothing about cables, nothing about speakers. But I learned — quickly.

They didn't tell me I would have to be a sound engineer.

I Would Have To Be A Producer.

When we went to sing in other churches, we needed risers. I had stood on risers all my life, having been active in the school choirs from elementary school forward. But they don't sell risers at the local department stores. What should I do? I learned.

They didn't tell me where to go for special music equipment.

Also, as we went around to those other churches, standing on our risers in the front of the church, I saw over and over that the lighting in most churches is lousy. I wanted the congregations to see the vitality in those kids' faces as they sang about the Jesus they had come to know and love so well. That's hard to do when the faces are in shadows.

So we needed some lighting. We needed portable lighting. I didn't know anything about that, either; but I learned.

They didn't tell me I would have to be a lighting expert.

We became a small rolling production company. It took lots of cars and vans and muscle to go from place to place. It was work, but it was fun.

One night we visited a little church on the far side of town from where our church was located. We rolled up in our caravan of vehicles and set up our risers, lights, sound reinforcement, electric bass guitar, electric lead guitar, acoustic guitars, and all our enthusiasm for a brief rehearsal.

Things were going great for a few minutes, but then all the lights went out. No electricity. We had blown a fuse. No lights, no sound, no electric guitars. We had grown in our little production so much that the average church could not handle our electrical needs.

They didn't tell me I would have to be an electrician, too.

As you can tell, I was gradually initiated into the production side of things with The Young Folk. Everything I had to do was fairly new to me, even though I had been a part of large productions in high school and college. It's just that in those past activities, somebody else had to worry about the lights and sound and stuff. I just performed.

* * *

Janet was now ready for her first job as a full-time minister of music. She had graduated near the top of her class from one of the leading schools in the country with a degree in church music.

She arrived at her new church in Nebraska during the last two weeks of August, giving her enough time to move in and adjust to her new community before starting her responsibilities right after Labor Day.

Things went very smoothly. She loved them; they loved her. She was really blessed to be working in such a large and active church for her very first job. There were nearly 1500 members in the church, and most of them were active.

The time came for her to plan her Christmas program, so she called a meeting of the music committee. What had they done before, and what would they like to do this year?

"Well, in the past we've done some Christmas cantatas. They've been fine, but we'd like to do more than just sing them. Over at the First Assembly, they really put on a great production each year. They have lights and costumes and… well, it's great! Lots of our own church people go over there to see it. Why can't we do something like that, too?"

So Janet had her marching orders. She was to produce an extravaganza. The only problem was that Janet had never done that before. She had seen a few, but she was never actually in one. And she certainly had never been responsible for all the details.

The first thing she needed was a musical that lent itself to that kind of production. She realized that she had better start looking right away because that search should have been completed during the summer.

Janet nearly lost her mind listening to all the new Christmas musicals the various publishing companies were promoting that fall. But she finally landed on one that would fill the bill.

Now where could she get costumes? Did the church own any lighting equipment? How would she amplify the main characters so that they could

I Would Have To Be A Producer.

be heard? Wouldn't microphones in front of Mary and Joseph look tacky? What about wireless mics? Should they use sets? If so, where would she get them?

It didn't take Janet long to realize that this undertaking might send her to the undertaker! She was in over her head, and she knew it.

So she went to see the senior pastor. Wonder what she expected him to know about such a production? But he seemed like the right person with whom to talk.

After she presented him with the picture — this is what they want me to do, but I'm not sure I know how to do it — he asked her a very simple question that took care of the whole problem.

"Well, Janet, how much is this going to cost? Do you have it in your music budget?"

Bong! She hadn't really thought of that. No, there was no extra money in this year's music budget to pay for sets, costumes, lights, sound reinforcement, and whatever else might be needed that she hadn't thought of yet. That settled it. She would just tell the committee that the church couldn't afford such a production this year. Maybe next year. Then there would be enough time to plan for it and do it right.

Janet was off the hook — at least for now. But something deep inside her said that she had better start planning for the following Christmas right now. She had a lot to learn.

When I started my first church job, it had been many years since the church had presented a special music service in the spring. I learned that the choir had tried to present some classical works with organ accompaniment. The attendance was so poor that it was embarrassing. As a result, they had given up on those types of presentations in favor of doing a great job with the Sunday morning worship music.

After I had been there for a few years, the choir had grown in size and ability. I began to get the itch to present something grand and with orchestra the following spring. I got permission and set out to have the choir offer Honegger's KING DAVID.

The Complainer in my choir assured me that it wouldn't work, being the pessimist that he was. That was all the challenge I needed: It *had* to work!

I got the conductor's score from the publisher. Now I was responsible to contract the professional orchestra that would accompany us.

They didn't tell me that I would have to be an orchestral contractor.

How many violins? Should I have as many second violins as first? I know I have to have a percussionist, but what instruments are these? I'd never heard of some of these things. And how many players will this take? Beats me.

I got through that trauma with the help of some instrumentalist friends who helped me with some of the decisions. The choir rehearsed passionately for many months, and the month of performance was rapidly nearing.

The senior pastor called me into his office. "How are the preparations going for this production?" he asked.

"Great!" I responded. "I think the choir is really into it, and I believe the people are going to love it."

But he wasn't returning my smiles of enthusiasm. He proceeded to tell me that he had reservations about the whole undertaking. Were we concentrating on a "performance" rather than a "worship service?" Would the Lord be honored in this, or would it be for the glory of me and the musicians involved?

They didn't tell me I would have to justify the presentation of great music as a worthy endeavor.

"Jerry, those are good questions," I offered, all the while wanting to kick him in his shins. "I believe you will be pleased. Why don't you plan to drop in on some rehearsals and see for yourself what the choir is learning and how this music tells the Biblical story so vividly?"

He smiled and assured me that he would consider doing that. To this day I don't know where his questions came from, but I am pretty sure that he was just reflecting to me some concerns that were brought to him by some other people. I wouldn't be at all surprised if one of those persons happened to be The Complainer. If he couldn't get to me directly with his comments, he could get the senior pastor to control me. Oh well, it didn't work.

I realized more than ever that this production had to succeed. And one of the primary ways it would be evaluated was for a large number of people to attend.

Considering the history that the church had for people not supporting presentations of this type — especially not classical music — I was a little worried.

I Would Have To Be A Producer.

What did I need to do to get them excited? Aha — the perfect idea. The role of the narrator in that oratorio is very central. Instead of getting one of the pastors or choir members to do it, I should get a celebrity. People love celebrities.

That was a very sneaky punch, but it worked. I remembered years earlier when I had heard Robert Reed narrate this work beautifully. Impeccably and reverently, in fact. Robert Reed is a television personality. Years ago, he was Mr. Brady of "The Brady Bunch" and the young attorney on a hit show in the 60's called "The Lawyers." He would be perfect.

They didn't tell me I would have to learn how to contact celebrities and enlist their aid.

Almost miraculously, it all came together. I reached Robert Reed, and he said yes. Now I had a trump card in my hand. People would love this.

But how would they know about it? I would need to advertise! That's it! And it had better be good quality advertising. After all, not many people can say that a Hollywood celebrity will be in our church tonight.

That led me to the next step — graphics. I would need eye-catching graphics for posters, ads, and for the printed programs. This was another new field for me. I had slept through art classes in school, but I could still do a pretty good job of kindergarten cut-and-paste.

They didn't tell me I would have to become a graphic artist.

Off to see the printer. What kind of paper did I want? How many ink colors? What colors? How many copies? Did I want to supply camera-ready artwork, or would I need their assistance? What about typesetting?

By the time I finished that project alone, my brain was fried. Decisions, decisions, decisions. And all about things that were basically new to me. I needed help. I needed experience. There was more to this producer thing than I realized.

The dress rehearsal finally came. It was a Saturday morning. Sitting in the balcony all alone was the senior pastor. He had not come to any of the rehearsals, except this one. Well, he won't stop us now — it's too late for that. I just hope he likes it.

The next morning in church, he stood in the pulpit and said, "Friends, yesterday I had the privilege of attending the dress rehearsal of the choir's presentation tonight of KING DAVID. I was thrilled! I can say to you that I believe this may be one of the most significant events ever to take place in this sanctuary!"

Boy, was I relieved. Nobody had asked him to say that: It came from his heart. He had been genuinely moved by the music and the whole presentation. I couldn't have asked for better PR.

Well, the time came, and it was a huge success. In fact, so many people attended that we had to turn some of them away. That was the beginning of many highly successful presentations of all types. We had to repeat most of them several times on consecutive nights because of the crowds surpassing the size of the sanctuary, and we had to add closed circuit TV as well.

That brought up a brand new problem — crowd control. I never expected that wonderful problem, but there it was. Should we sell tickets, or should we perhaps have free, reserved seats? New problems — new solutions needed.

By the way, the worst part of the whole experience was after it was over. That's when all the bills arrived. It was more expensive than I thought it would be. It was more expensive than the budget allowed. I had not done a great job of projecting the costs in advance, and my face was red. How the future productions would be financed was the subject of our next music committee meeting.

Does it ever end?

***

Remember that I told you about taking my teen choir — The Young Folk, on summer tours. I learned so much from those experiences — some of them by making big mistakes. I've put together a cassette tape entitled "How to Take Your Choir on Tour — Happily." There's information at the end of this book on how you can order that tape and other titles as well.

But something else grew out of the touring experience: I became the host in my own church for traveling musicians. Sometimes they were church choirs just like my own, out on the road for the summer tour experience. Sometimes they were Christian recording artists, coming through our city to minister.

In each case, there were differences and similarities. There were questions about lighting, sound, accompanying instruments, electricity, advertising, finances, and crowd control.

Some people are well organized. Others amaze me with their loosie-goosie ways of doing things. I found myself repeatedly having to take care of hosting details that no one had equipped me to do — except experience. You will, too.

Some Solutions

WHAT DO YOU NEED TO LEARN ABOUT in order to be a producer in your church for the simple and not-so-simple presentations that will come along. To start, you will need to understand lighting, recording, sound reinforcement, electricity, carpentry, costuming, makeup, multimedia, graphics, printing, financing, crowd control, and patience.

You will need to learn such terms as omnidirectional microphones, equalizers, ellipsoidals, watts, pancake, glue, 60-pound offset, screening, faders, and patience.

You will need to discover the joys of mid-range, snakes, dimmer boards, circular saws, eye liner, gels, feedback, matt finish, tape hiss, Styrofoam, wireless mics, and patience.

You can certainly see by now that there could be a whole series of manuals and indeed volumes of books written on just about all of these topics. It's a little overwhelming.

But never despair. What you need to learn, you will learn. Little by little, you will get the experience you need.

One of the most important terms for you to learn in this entire discussion is one simple word spelled d-e-l-e-g-a-t-e.

No, you don't have to do it all yourself. In fact, if you try to do it all, you're crazy. There will be lots of men and women in your choir — well, at least several — who will have some knowledge, some expertise, and some willingness in one or more of these areas.

If you don't know the answers, ask. They kept telling us that in school, but we adults sometimes allow our pride from allowing us to reveal ignorance.

Many times I have asked for a volunteer to help with an aspect of a presentation only to discover that the guy who raised his hand and said he would take it on had never actually had any experience in that area. Amazing! But you know what: Those guys who are willing are also resourceful enough to find out what they need to know in order to do the job and do it well. It's taken some faith on my part to turn over some projects to inexperienced Willie, but the results have always been more than adequate.

Could You Speak a Little Louder, Please?
A good sound system is one of your most important acquisitions.

If people can't hear it, they'll stay home. If they can hear it, but it crackles and distorts until their skeletons rattle, they ought to stay home.

One of the most important acquisitions any church can make is an excellent sound system. That investment is one that is absolutely basic to a successful worship experience and to your whole music program.

If you find your church wanting in this area, you need to start planting seeds immediately. And watch out, because when they agree, you will probably be tapped to do the research and recommendation on what to purchase.

There are two things about church sound system acquisitions that I have found to be universal. Be armed with this information so that you can steer your committee correctly.

First, churches just don't want to spend the amount of money that they ought. Excellent sound system installations are not cheap. Average ones are cheap; excellent ones are expensive.

I Would Have To Be A Producer.

Second, many laymen only think of the amplification of the preacher's voice when they think about their sound needs. Their only concern is being able to hear the spoken word. You will need to help them understand that they should be prepared to amplify all types of music as well. That might include amplification for the entire choir, for soloists and small ensembles, for a piano and probably other instruments, and possibly for the playback of accompaniment tapes.

Rob is a sound engineer. He often writes a column in my newsletter, MUSIC REVELATION, called "Sound Advice," and he has been extremely helpful as a consultant to churches researching their sound needs.

Rob tells a story of a large church who engaged his services. They got five bids on their new sound system. The lowest bid was for $12,000, and the highest bid was for $28,000. The next to the lowest bid was $18,000, and all the rest were in the twenties.

Rob made a recommendation that the church did not accept. You can probably guess what they did. Yes, the cheaper-is-better mentality won the day, and they opted for the $12,000 system.

Rob was not happy, but they thought they were pretty smart.

During the months and indeed the years following the installation of that system, Rob tells me that the church has called him over and over for help. They needed extra equipment almost every time the choir made a special presentation. Things didn't work right during the morning services, so they had to be repaired or sometimes replaced with better equipment.

The end result was that this church finally spent *more* than $28,000 correcting their mistake. They should have done it right the first time, but they were too stubborn.

Rob tells me that this example is echoed all over. You will probably find it difficult to lead your church to spend what they ought to spend the first time out, but you should try.

Another very common, very stupid mistake that many churches make with the installation of their sound reinforcement is that they will try to hide the equipment and its operator in a sound room somewhere adjacent to the sanctuary. The operator may or may not be able to see what is going on in the sanctuary, so a discreet glass window or closed circuit TV are often his sight line.

As he sits in that little room, he listens on headphones to what is happening. That is a terrible mistake. Whether he is in the room or not, it is impossible for that sound operator to hear what is really happening by listening through headphones. The result will be microphones not on when the pastor begins talking or when the soloist begins her song, frequent feedback, inadequate volume for the layperson reading Scripture, and all sorts of other aggravations.

Fight for it and win: The sound operator needs to be inside the room with you, hearing what is happening with his own ears. The best location is for him to be centrally located in the rear of the room, if possible.

It seems that most rooms have dead spots, acoustically speaking. Your sanctuary is probably no exception. Make sure that your sound operator is not located in one of the room's dead spots. That's another common mistake.

When the time comes for you to upgrade or replace your sound system, call in experts. Have someone measure the room with electronic equipment so that they can tell you the acoustical qualities of your sanctuary.

Get references for the company that interests you. Go to a location like yours where they have made an installation. Check it out, and ask the people there if they have been happy not only with the results of the installation, but with the follow-up help they received after the installation was made.

Most experts will tell you that the best arrangement in most sanctuaries is a central cluster of speakers, suspended from the ceiling over and slightly to the front of the worship area. The alternative is to dispense speakers throughout the room. This is not as good, because the psychological focal point of the sound source is lost. With a central cluster, it is easier to give the illusion that all of the sound is emanating from the front.

Once you have succeeded in getting the best installation possible for your church, get some training in how to use it. In fact, it is important that you get a number of people trained to use it properly. It's silly to purchase a $25,000 car and turn it over to a ten-year-old to drive! Having competently trained sound technicians in your congregation is essential. You should be one of them.

I have had great success with teen-aged boys and young men as sound operators. They seem to have an interest in this sort of thing, and they take it seriously. Just don't allow them to tamper with the equipment: They can really foul it up if they get knob happy.

You may have the need for some portable sound equipment as well, especially if you have an ensemble that sings anywhere outside of the sanctuary. If you have a touring group, then a portable system is essential.

Go shopping. Wherever they sell guitars and other supplies for rock musicians, they also sell great portable sound systems. Tell them what you want the equipment for, and they will guide you in the right direction. By the way, if you will be using the equipment for much travel, be sure to tell them that. Some sound systems stand up under bumps and bangs better than others.

You Light Up My Life
Good lighting is often overlooked in planning for worship services.

It seems like those people who are gifted with architectural design in the church just don't have a sense of what constitutes good lighting for worship services. If they can generally flood an area with light, they are satisfied.

I've lost track of the number of times I've been sitting in the sanctuary at a Sunday morning service and have been distracted by the shadows or glares on peoples' faces. That includes the pastor's face as well. There have been a few churches where the pastor looked as if he were being lit for a Halloween show.

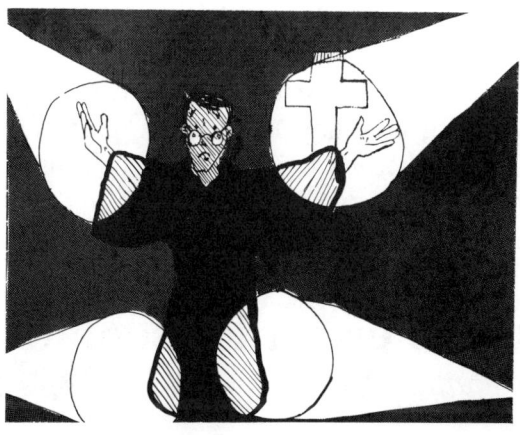

One of the most common problems is that the sanctuary has a high ceiling. The people are sitting at a level lower than the pulpit and choir loft, so they are looking up. The lights in the high ceiling shine down right into their eyes. Now I have sensitive eyes, so the result of such a setting for me is a giant headache.

Go into your sanctuary some night with two or three other people. Have them stand in the key places that are focal points during your worship services. Move around the room and sit in various places yourself to see the results. If you discover an abundance of glare or perhaps too many shadows, it's time to call in a lighting expert to come over and give you some advice.

The installation of supplemental lighting in your sanctuary need not be all that expensive. If you have an electrician in your church — which is fairly common — he can probably do the installation for you at very reasonable rates.

The ability to control all your lighting with rheostats is highly recommended. There are many times during the church year or during your special presentations when you can make excellent use of dramatically controlled lighting. So even if you don't find the need to replace or supplement your existing lighting, look into adding rheostats to what you do have.

Again, there are great portable systems. Ask for information on fresnels, ellipsoidals, lighting trees, and dimmer boards. Call the drama teacher at your local high school and ask if he or she can give you some tips on the best use of colored lighting gels. Which ones are best for skin tones? Which ones are the most exciting? Where can you purchase them?

Use dramatic lighting in your special music presentations. Don't be afraid of the accusation that it's too theatrical. If Jesus were to come to America today, I suspect He would make use of all the tools available to Him to communicate the gospel.

Picture Perfect Presentations
The use of multimedia greatly enhances your message.

As we have said before, people tend to remember more of what they see than what they hear. So the use of multimedia in some of your presentations is definitely an asset.

I Would Have To Be A Producer.

This is ultimately another category for the experts, but it doesn't take too much experience to set up a slide projector and screen. The real fun comes in finding the right slides to use and coordinating them to the music.

Several guys introduced me to the creative use of slides. And I'm glad I didn't try this one on my own, because it took a tremendous amount of time to bring it off.

We were doing Gaither's HIS LOVE REACHING for Christmas one year. It's an expressive work that naturally lends itself to visual representation.

We asked all the members of the choir to look back at their old vacation slides to see if they had any outstanding nature scenes or interesting faces of people that they would like to share with us. We got more than we could use.

But we were still in need of some special slides — pictures that were hard to find. That's when I learned that there are companies that do nothing but photo research and who will rent slides to you. I found them by letting my fingers do the walking. That information came in very handy later on when I needed to produce an album cover for a recording I did with my ensemble.

By the way, if you don't have such resources where you live, contact a good graphic art studio or an advertising agency in town. They will probably know where you can go to rent great slides.

After literally months of looking, we finally found all the slides we needed. The next question was how many screens to use. The decision was made to use three screens with two projectors on each. I was getting more and more excited.

When we sat down to listen to the recording and try to figure out just what slide would go where, these guys convinced me that my expectations were so complicated that they needed a computer to run the whole thing — literally. I thought they were telling me it couldn't be done, but they were simply saying that we needed to rent a common piece of equipment called a programmer that would take over and run those six slide projectors for me.

We were using the accompaniment tape anyway. Codes are placed onto the tape on a separate track that tell the computer programmer what to do. That way the slides are perfectly timed with the music, and there's no embarrassing human error.

Several very neat things that you can do with these slides have to do with decay. You can cause one slide to dissolve on the screen either rapidly or very, very slowly. The next slide sort of melts into view rather than jumping onto the screen as it does in a home slide show. Beautiful.

In later productions, I learned the joy of rear-screen projection. That's much more professional and impressive than having to place slide projectors out in the sanctuary for everyone to see and hear.

In this day and age, don't overlook video projection either — both front and rear screen. You can do amazing things with video, playing it back in regular speed, sped up, or in slow motion. Wild.

And if you have a *big* budget, look into lasers. Depicting the Resurrection with lasers is awesome!

But I Didn't Know Anything About It
*Proper advertising is necessary in order
to get people to attend.*

If you are going to go to the trouble to make a major presentation, or if you are going to host a touring group or well-known Christian artist, you must learn some of the basics of good advertising. And don't forget to allow enough money in your budget for advertising, either. It's essential.

Did you know some people say that in business, more than half the expense should be in advertising? I've heard some say that a good, strong, growing business will allow 65% of its expenses to go into advertising.

That may not be necessary for you in the church music ministry — after all, you almost have a built-in audience. But advertise you must.

Here is an important rule of thumb from the advertising community. People have to see something at least *three* times before they have seen it once. In other words, if you are using written bulletin announcements as your primary means of advertising, you need to run the announcements at least three weeks before the average person will see it one time. That, of course, assumes that they read the bulletin announcements at all!

In your church you have several other means of getting the word out. Most churches have a church newspaper. Use it. But remember the three-time principle.

You should make posters or have them professionally printed. Hang them in enough places around the church that people will see them at least three times, or they'll be missed. Put them on the doors entering the rest rooms: Almost everybody goes in there! Put them above the water

I Would Have To Be A Producer.

fountains. Hang them on the walls so that they are seen when entering and leaving the building. Send them with your choir members to their places of employment. Get them all over town. The more places your own church members see them around town, the more interested they will become in supporting what is happening at their own church.

One mistake some churches make is requiring posters to be placed only on certain bulletin boards. Lots of those bulletin boards are never read.

Use the local newspaper. If possible, find some angle of your event that makes an interesting story. It may be the appearance of a special guest. It may be the first time your community has seen lasers. Perhaps it will have to do with the fact that you are combining with another church for a joint venture, promoting community cooperation and interest.

Then write a story for the newspaper. Use short paragraphs and lots of names of people. Send in a black and white glossy photograph of something that they can use with the story. That will greatly increase your chances of having it printed. Type it double spaced, and put "For Immediate Release" at the top of the page.

All that will hopefully get you a feature article that won't require you to take out a paid ad in the newspaper. Those ads are expensive both to produce and to run.

All radio and television stations are required to feature a certain amount of publicity for community groups — especially non-profit groups — called

Public Service Announcements. These PSA's are free. All you have to do is type the copy, double spaced, and mail it to the station. They decide when they will run it. Be sure to include the essentials in a very brief statement — what, when, where. They don't give a lot of time to PSA's.

Then you might consider paying for some advertising on radio or television. The most economical air time available is on Christian radio. I've known top secular radio stations to charge exactly ten times the amount for one 60-second advertisement as a Christian station. Of course the listening audience on the secular station is usually larger. If you are trying to reach the non-churched with your event, you will need to consider that.

Print a small flyer based on the artwork of your poster and include it as an insert in your Sunday morning worship bulletin. It's best to do that one or two weeks prior to the event. That flyer is much more effective than just putting in a bulletin announcement.

With all of that activity, there are still your two strongest sources of advertising yet to tap. One of those is your choir itself. Nobody is going to have more interest in having people attend than your choir members. If they are excited about the work you are doing, then you need to encourage them to get busy and talk it up. Have them invite the people at their office. Invite the neighbors on their street. Invite their relatives who don't go to your church. If you sell tickets, then it's easier for your choir to advertise: They will accomplish that as they pound the pavement.

The last and most helpful source of all is your pastor. Now I hate it when verbal announcements in church are placed in the service in a way that they interrupt our worship. So please don't misunderstand me when I say that you need to encourage your pastor to make an announcement for you.

In spite of the fact that people tend to remember more of what they see than what they hear, the church poses one notable exception. People will remember what the pastor says before they will remember what is written in the bulletin. Get him on your side in advertising your event.

So you need to organize your advertising campaign to use all of the resources available to you. Perhaps you should establish an advertising committee for each event. Just be sure to budget for it and allow enough time for it to take effect.

Let Me Illustrate

Get to know the basics of graphic arts and printing.

All those posters, flyers, and printed programs that go along with special productions don't just happen. Somebody has to pull out the paper, ink, rulers, and creativity to bring them into being. That someone just might be you.

No, you don't have to be an artist to bring this off, but it helps, of course. This is yet another area where finding talented people in your church to help you is the smart way to go.

But there is much that can and should be done "in house" in order to give you control over your publications and to save you lots of shekels.

If your church is ready for the computer age, you ought to ask them to get you a laser printer. With or without desktop publishing software, you can turn out some very handsome stuff on a laser printer that the layman will think was typeset.

There are many sources of good clip art. That's the artwork that is published for the purpose of your clipping it out of the book and pasting it into your own publication. You can find good clip art everywhere. Just start looking through your magazines at home and envision how you might use this or that piece of graphic art.

Make yourself a lighting board. All you need is a simple wooden box without a top on it. Purchase a piece of plexiglass and cut it to fit the top. Place a cheap flourescent light inside, and you're in business.

Why a lighting board? Because you use it to paste up your headlines, text, and clip art. Go to your local office or art supply store and purchase some graph paper. Tape it to the top of your lighting board and use the lines on it as a guide for the paste up work you do. Nobody likes crooked headlines.

If you have a good art supply store handy, go visit them and discover two very wonderful tools that will be of great joy to you. One of them is graphic tape. You can purchase straight lines in various widths, ornate borders, and all sorts of symbols clearly printed in black onto transparent tape. Place that on your artwork and you're beginning to enter the world of the professionals.

The second item is a hand waxer. Never again use rubber cement for your paste-up work. It's a real pain. Waxers are not expensive and are far more convenient for you to use. These little electric gadgets heat up just enough to melt little squares of special wax you purchase to go in them. When the wax becomes liquid, you roll it onto the rear of the paper or art that you want to paste down. It immediately solidifies, but it doesn't become really hard. You place the artwork down where you want it and burnish it with a small tool or roller. The beauty of this method, however, is that you can easily pick up the waxed art and move it anywhere you like, then just burnish it again. That's impossible with rubber cement.

When the budget allows, get yourself a professional waxer for a few hundred dollars. It will save you an enormous amount of time.

With your lighting board, some graphic tape, carefully chosen clip art, and hopefully a laser printer, you will be able to produce camera-ready artwork at a fraction of the normal cost.

What is camera-ready artwork? When you take your work into the print shop, they usually photograph it and actually print it from the negative. If it's camera-ready, you don't have to pay them to do the paste-up, etc. Great savings.

Get to know a good local printer personally. You will need lots of help and advice to end up with the best creations. And printers are notorious for making lots of mistakes. You will need to allow plenty of time for your printing job just in case it has to be corrected. Believe me, you will have some of those times.

Ask your printer to show you some different kinds of paper and explain the differences to you. There will be times when you will want 20-lb. bond, other times when you will need 60-lb. offset, and still other times when you will prefer text weight or index stock. He'll walk you through that quickly.

Also ask to see a book that shows you the effect of screening different ink colors. If you print a color in 100%, then you get the full, solid color. But the printer can "screen" any color in different percentages. This is done by printing hundreds or thousands of tiny dots in that color, giving the effect of various shades.

It costs much more to print something in two ink colors or more, but you can use only one ink color with various screens and create the illusion of multiple colors. For instance, you can print dark emerald green letters within a bordered box that uses a 20% screen of the emerald green as its background. The effect is very striking.

As I said, ask the printer to show you a book that reveals the various levels of screening and their appearance in relation to one another. Then you can have some real fun.

Tickets Please
*You can best control your attendance
and costs by issuing tickets.*

Many churches adopt the idea of tickets for their special events. The primary reason is crowd control. It's very, very helpful to know in advance approximately how many folks are planning to show up.

You don't have to charge money for the tickets. In fact, some churches would frown heavily on that idea. But even a free ticket can be a yardstick by which you measure your expected attendance.

The financing of major presentations is always a problem. They are very expensive, you know. While many churches are willing to put the costs into the budget, the vast majority of them prefer to take up an offering at the event itself to help defray the expenses.

Personally, I have no problem with charging for tickets. But if that's not to be, I certainly have no problem with taking up an offering. I can tell you from experience that it's white knuckle time until that offering is counted. Will it be enough? Will it be enough?

You would be better off to convince your church to budget for all the expenses and then take the ticket sale money or the offering money and put it into the church's budget. Or perhaps they would consider a revolving account that's just for major presentations. If you get more in offerings than you need this time around, let it go into next year's presentations. If too little this year, tap that special fund.

You might also consider sponsors for these events. If your church will allow this idea, it's very helpful to have individuals in the church make specific donations into the Special Presentations Fund.

We're Gonna Be Famous
Every choir ought to record at some point in their life.

Your choir members, or your ensemble for that matter, will probably love the idea of recording. They'll become stars! And the members of the congregation enjoy having such recordings to play in their homes or in their cars.

If you find yourself in the record producing business, there are a few things you need to know.

Most people prefer cassette tapes to record albums. In fact, many record producing companies today won't be producing any more albums — just cassettes and compact disks.

Recording the choir may be done using multiple-track recorders. With an eight-track machine, for instance, you may record simultaneously or separately eight different programs.

That means that the sopranos may be on track one, the altos on two, the tenors on three, and the basses on four. That still leaves you four empty tracks for accompanying instruments or soloists.

You may record the accompaniment at one time and the voices at another. There are real advantages both ways, but you will have greater control over the final recording if you do it separately.

After you've recorded everything, you still have the artistic task of mixing. That means that you will go with your recording engineer to a place where you can hear all eight tracks played back simultaneously. If you need more tenor on that line, you kick them up higher. If the basses goof in that measure, you can cover them up for a few moments.

You can also add some electronic enhancements during the mixing time such as reverberation. That's the wonderful singing-in-the-bathtub sound that we wish we had every Sunday morning. Or you might want to refer to it as the cathedral sound, with stone walls and stained glass surrounding you.

I Would Have To Be A Producer.

It is better to record the choir and accompaniment in a room that is dead acoustically, then add reverb later. That way you have much more control. If you record in a room that is alive, you will always have to live with the sound that goes on the tape the first time around.

After your sound engineer knows exactly how you want the tape to be mixed, he masters it onto another tape. This master tape is what is used to reproduce your albums or cassettes. You send that master tape to a business that specializes in that product. Again, let your fingers do the walking. It doesn't hurt to ask someone you know for a recommendation, because there is a real difference in quality among these businesses.

The musical selections that you choose for your recording may be covered by copyright laws. If they are, then you may indeed record them, but you will need what is called a mechanical license. Here's what you do. Write to the publisher of each title. Tell them that you would like to have a standard mechanical license for each piece of theirs that you will be recording.

They will automatically send you a simple form. You will fill it out and send them a check which is the royalty you are paying for the right to record their material. It is illegal for you to record without that agreement, so don't break the law!

The amount you have to pay for a mechanical license is very small. The laws change from time to time, and the amount gradually increases. But in general, you will be asked to pay only a few cents for each title times the number of copies of albums or tapes you produce. Notice that it's not the number of copies you *sell*, but the number you actually manufacture. So figure this cost into your budget from the start.

So far we've talked you through the basics of being a producer of a recording without bringing up the part that usually takes the most time and causes the most headaches. That's the artwork that will go with that finished product.

If you are talking about a record album, you are considering a greater expense for graphics and printing than if you are talking about a cassette tape. But in either case, get started on the artwork at the beginning of the project. If you know what the order of the songs will be in the final product, then get the printing tasks under way immediately. You will spend more time proofing, correcting, and waiting on the artwork than you ever thought possible. It will hold up your project by months if you don't do it right.

Your Place or Mine?
Being a good host for guest musicians takes some thoughtfulness.

In all this discussion about being a producer, I've mentioned taking your group on tour or hosting a group/individual at your place. So to close out this section, I want to give you some pointers that I hope will earn you the reputation of the best church to visit. Let's take it all from the angle of your being the host church. You can certainly adapt these ideas and send them to any church that might be hosting you in the future. After all, you want done unto you what you are willing to do for others, right?

Whether they asked you to allow them to come or you picked up the phone and invited them, you owe your guests the courtesy of advertising their event as if it were your own. So all that we said about informing the people in your church and community applies here as well.

If you are receiving a group, they will probably need food and housing for the night. Get started early with the housing list: It takes time. And be very sure to have at least three alternative homes on that list because some bozo or three will surely let you down at the last minute. To be fair, those times are usually for good reasons; but I'm amazed at how many times well-intentioned individuals just "forget" that this was the night they had promised their spare room to a couple of hungry, tired kids.

Establish two copies of the housing list. Keep one in your files. Give the other one to the visiting director. There are many possible needs for that list. The most common one is that somebody will leave something behind, and you may be the person turned to for help.

Are you sure about the homes you are using? I've known of a few times when alcohol was served to minors or when someone got just a little too friendly with someone else.

I can also identify with a few rare occasions when I've been on tour, was taken to my host home by an absolutely delightful host, only to discover that the facilities were the pits. In one home the bed sheets were so filthy that I had to ask for clean ones before I could go to bed. We were both embarrassed, but at least I slept better.

Once you have your housing list all arranged, make out a 3 x 5 card for each host, listing the names of their house guests. Give it to them as they are meeting one another that night. Make out another 3 x 5 card for

I Would Have To Be A Producer.

one of the guests listing the host and hostess name, their home address and telephone number. This is very, very helpful for getting to know one another, finding the way back to the home after a party if they get lost, and for keeping you out of the middle when someone left their brown sweater behind. It's also handy for the guests who will wish to write a thank-you note later.

Here's a little touch that will make a good impression right off the bat. Have some trays of fruit juice all poured and ready for them when they arrive. What a delightful surprise it will be for them, and their spirits will be lifted for the entire stay.

They are going to be a hungry bunch, and you will probably only have time to feed them a meal at the church. If there is indeed time to have them go to the host homes, great. But if you are the chef, please remember that they have probably existed on fast food while on the road. In addition to that, most of the churches that have been feeding them during their tour will give them fried chicken, spaghetti, or sloppy Joes. They will really appreciate a well-balanced meal that includes salad and fruit. Watch their eyes light up when they enter the fellowship hall and see some thoughtfulness behind the cooking.

Check the restrooms. They are about to be invaded by a hoard of travelers. Have an extra supply of paper towels and toilet paper in all the church's restrooms. They will love you for it.

Get some sweet hostesses to show people around when they have questions, or be sure to post some signs for them. A strange building laid out like an ancient pyramid is intimidating to a newcomer, believe me.

Set up a private room for the director to place his or her things and where they can change their clothes. They deserve the luxury: They are working extra hard on this trip.

Be sure to set up the dressing rooms for your guests with paper over the windows. Don't forget the glass window in the door, if you have one. It's tough on the kids to have to all go into the rest room to change into their outfits before the service. It's too crowded and too hot.

Arrange for security in those dressing rooms. Lock them. If necessary, hire a guard or two. A wonderful visit can be ruined by one stolen wallet.

If your budget can afford it, and even if it can't, arrange a motel for the director. If there are other adult chaperons on the trip, it would be lovely if you could do the same for them. They will love the privacy — finally — and the good night's sleep that the motel will offer them. It's like an oasis.

If you are hosting teen-agers, they love to party afterwards, and they love pizza. Nobody has yet determined in which order these items should appear on the list, but if you can combine the two in one event, you are a real winner. All that depends, of course, on the timing of the worship service. If you can start early enough to put this pizza party into the schedule as well, great.

Just remember that those kids have to get to their host homes at a decent hour. And the hostess there will probably have baked a pie or cake for them to consume that night. If you are going to have a party, be very sure to communicate that fact to the hostess well in advance. If transportation to the host homes is going to be a real problem, you'd be wiser to skip the party. After all, you don't want to inconvenience that hostess on whom you will probably be calling again in the future.

Pick up some little snacks for the group to take along as their bus pulls out the following morning. Almost anything will do — it's the thought that counts.

And when it's time to say farewell, get onto the bus with them, share your joy at their visit, and pray for them. You will have just met some new folks who just may become life-long friends.

CHAPTER
6

THEY DIDN'T TELL ME

◆ ◆ ◆

I Would Need To Be A Bible Scholar.

The Situation

I HAD BEEN ON THE STAFF OF THE CHURCH for just a few weeks. There were naturally many new things I was learning. One of them was that staff meetings were too long, but they were considered very important.

Being the new kid on the block, I mostly listened. One of the things I heard over and over was what the Bible had to say about this or that. The Scriptures were applied to almost all the decision making.

Several of the issues being discussed were pretty heavy, such as divorce and remarriage. These were intriguing discussions.

I had gone to a church-related college years earlier, and one of my required courses was the Bible. I had been completely through the Old Testament and the New Testament during those years, so I figured that I had just about all the Bible I needed.

But as these questions kept coming before the staff, I felt dumb. I didn't have the slightest idea just exactly how Jesus responded to divorce, and I certainly didn't remember Paul's teachings on women in positions of authority.

As I was contemplating my ignorance in my listening mode during the third meeting, the pastor turned to me and said, "Harry, why don't you lead our staff devotions next Tuesday?"

Panic! The pastors, the secretaries, the custodians, and all the volunteer members of our large church gathered in a meeting room for 30 minutes once a week for this time of spiritual food. I thought only the ordained clergy types would be the leaders. I discovered that all full-time staff members took a turn. My ignorance was to be put on public display next Tuesday!

Well, I wasn't all that ignorant. I remembered more than I'm giving myself credit for. It's just that I had not actively used the Bible for so long. Oh well, get to work.

I did a good job. Is it OK for me to say that? I mean I really surprised myself. That little time of study and sharing built some needed confidence in me. I actually enjoyed it. But it did point out to me rather abruptly just how much I needed to study the Bible in order to recall some of the things I had learned about it years earlier.

Joining the staff the same day as I was Dr. R.C. Sproul. This man and his wife, Vesta, became great friends to Elizabeth and me. We spent lots of time together talking and laughing.

R.C. is one of the most knowledgeable and gifted Bible expositors I have ever heard. People all over the church were talking about his inspired teaching. The Scriptures came to life from his lips in ways that astounded me. No other person has sparked the desire in me to study and know the Word of God like R.C. Sproul.

I will never forget one of R.C.'s early sermons at the church. His text was Hosea 4:6 which reads, "My people are destroyed from lack of knowledge." Amen, I thought. You see, I was feeling pretty good because I had done a great 30-minute devotional from the Bible last Tuesday.

But something told me that I'd better do some more preparation: That one devotional couldn't last forever.

So I set aside some time in my office each morning with the book of Matthew and several commentaries that were left over from college days. I also bought a few more reference books that R.C. had recommended.

It was actually fun. I mean I was receiving new insights every day from the Gospel of Matthew, and I was enjoying it!

I will always remember a very simple little conversation I had with the senior pastor in the hallway. "How are things going, Harry? How are you and the Lord doing?"

"Super, Jerry. By the way, I've been studying the book of Matthew every morning. It's been really neat."

"That's great," he said. But then he became more serious, leaned towards me and added, "That will stay with you and equip you for the future."

That sentence could have been delivered with background music and dramatic lighting. For some reason it spoke to my spirit. Yes, he's right. This is the kind of thing that lasts.

I Would Need To Be A Bible Scholar.

*
**

We were having a great choir rehearsal and breezing right along through a stirring arrangement of "All Hail the Power of Jesus' Name."

One of my favorite things to do with a choir is to highlight word meanings. I believe that many words have feelings and colors associated with them. If you can get the choir to embrace those feelings and express those colors, the singing will have tremendously more empathy than otherwise.

So I was giving the choir some encouragement on the feelings and colors of the word "power." They were loving it. So I helped them see angels falling prostrate before the Lord in heaven. Another surge of energy filled their singing.

It was fun and challenging to ask the question, "What does it mean to crown Him Lord of *all*?" We shared some thoughts, and then we sang it again.

All through the song I had done a great job of displaying my enlightened understanding of this marvelous old hymn, and the choir was eating it up.

Then Jack raised his hand in the tenor section. Jack was one of my favorite people in the whole church. He was in his early twenties, worked with the young people, always smiled, and he was always there if you needed him for anything.

"Yes Jack?"

"I was wondering, Harry, what is a 'diadem'?"

"A diadem?" I repeated the word as a question. I knew I had heard the word somewhere before, but at that moment I couldn't tell you where.

"Yeah. We just sang 'bring forth the royal diadem.' What is that?"

Suddenly all my pride and ego were reduced to ground beef. I was on the spot. Having felt as if I were king of the mountain on my little podium, leading all these people to so powerfully sing that great hymn, at this moment my buddy Jack had sabotaged me. Well, he didn't do it on purpose: He was honestly curious.

But I didn't know. Someone else in the choir raised her hand. "It's a crown of some type, isn't it? I believe it's a crown. Maybe it's Middle Eastern or something. But it means that Jesus has authority."

Made sense to me. Whatever it was, we were going to use it to crown Him. So I thanked her for the information and promised to research the question for a later time. That experience helped teach me a lesson about my knowledge of the texts we sing.

Later, when we were singing "A Mighty Fortress Is Our God," I scurried to a dictionary to look up "Sabaoth." I was hoping somebody would stop the rehearsal and ask me what a "Sabaoth" was so that I could feel a little pride in displaying my knowledge. Nobody did. So I asked them if anyone knew what it meant. Silence. It just underscored the fact that folks tend to sing through those texts with their minds turned off. By the way, do you know what it means? You should!

It wasn't long after that the choir was rehearsing Handel's MESSIAH. My wife was singing in the choir at the time, and she was also taking a wonderful Bible course called The Bethel Series under the masterful teaching of R.C. Sproul.

At dinner one night, she asked me, "Are you going to tell the choir what it means when they are singing 'And He shall purify the sons of Levi'?"

I looked at her for a moment, wondering if the expression on my face was revealing the fact that I couldn't answer the question at all. She might as well have asked me to explain electricity, because nothing was coming to my mind.

I brilliantly responded, "What do you mean?"

She immediately revealed not only an understanding of that text, but a real excitement about it. She was learning so much from R.C.'s teaching. She and I often enjoyed talking about different things in the Bible.

After listening to her for a few minutes, I said, "I know what — Why don't you share this information with the choir next Wednesday. I think they ought to hear this."

I could see it in her eyes. I had said the right thing. She did share, and I could see little lights come on above the heads of lots of folks around the room. They even thanked her for sharing, and then we sang it one more time — with feeling.

Every choir has at least one person within it who is "The Judge." Remember that character? For him everything is either black or white, and he has lots of opinions to share.

My most recent Judge did a flip over a portion of the text in a musical that I was conducting. It's a great musical called EL SHADDAI. I could tell that the choir was absolutely connected to the work.

But then a letter came from one of the members. She was most disturbed about a phrase in the work that reads, "If you have seen the Father, then you have seen the Son." That was not Scriptural, and she refused to sing it. In fact, her husband had told her to drop out of the choir because of it.

I had dinner with her and her husband. She did drop out of the choir because we agreed to disagree. For her, these words were a distortion of Christ's teachings that no man has seen the Father.

I shared with her my conviction that there was indeed room for poetic license, that the following phrase in the text clarified the intention ("If you have seen the Father, then you have seen the Son; for the ancient God of Israel and Calvary are one."), and that the word "seen" was not intended to be taken literally. We were also singing at that time an arrangement of "Great Is Thy Faithfulness" in which we say "morning by morning, new mercies I see." I pointed out that we don't actually see mercies with our physical eyes in that text.

But she preferred black or white — no grays. I thought the text was a clever expression that could help the Jewish person see Jesus Christ as Messiah, but she saw it as heresy.

They didn't tell me I would need to be a Biblical scholar.

***

In our church we had a group of laypersons who were committed to good adult Christian education. They loved the Bible and the pursuit of knowledge about our Lord, so they started a great program called The Christian Lay Academy (CLA).

Classes of all types that related to the Christian life were offered, and hundreds of adults came out all nights of the week to study one subject or another.

One of the goals of the leaders of the CLA was that each and every full-time staff member of our church would teach on the faculty as often as possible. So every few months, as plans were being laid for the next round of classes, I would receive a phone call from Rick or JoAnn.

"Hi, Harry. I'm calling about the CLA next term. We would like for you to teach a class. Can we count on you?"

Realizing that the teacher learns more than the student, and knowing that having the responsibility would drive me to study the Bible more diligently, I said yes — not every time they called, but often enough.

I chose a short New Testament book for my first outing — the book of Colossians. It was a time of super growth for me as I dug into that book. The more I studied what others had to say about Paul's writings, the more I wanted to know.

You can't imagine how glad I was that I had studied Colossians when one of my choir members made an appointment to see me for counseling. She was having a real problem with astrology. Is it right or wrong? Does God condemn it or condone it?

I Would Need To Be A Bible Scholar.

There was no difficulty in my being able to turn to the book of Colossians and share with her what God has to say there on the subject. Having been exposed to that brief passage on astrology, I had been led in my studies to other Scriptures on the same theme. So I was equipped to help her from a Biblical perspective.

Never would I have dreamed in my former school of music that some day I would be sitting with a person in my office giving them counsel for their life based on the Word of God.

Having had such a good experience with the Colossians class, I was willing to tackle other books and other subjects along the way; and I will never regret the time and energy put into those studies and teachings. They have helped equip me to be a better choir director as I deal with Biblically based texts week in and week out. And they have helped me with the task of spiritual guidance for those who come to me seeking it.

The Young Folk, that teen choir I've talked about, met on Thursday nights. As I shared earlier, when I first met these kids, they were the most committed Christians I had ever encountered.

When we got together for rehearsals, they wanted to pray. I did, too, but they were actually the leaders — not me.

Besides praying, they wanted to share. That helped them become a "family", which I believe every choir needs to do at some level or another.

And above all, they wanted to keep the Word of God active in their lives. One of the leaders of that group was a high-school senior by the name of Doug. He's now a leading Presbyterian pastor in California. Doug was not the only person to come out of that group and go into full-time Christian work. There were several other pastors, musicians, and mission workers being formed by God in that marvelous body of kids.

In their rap sessions, as we called them, they would bring up many questions about life as only teen-agers can. Having been through those interesting years myself not that long before, I was equipped to intelligently discuss many of their concerns. When it came to the Biblical questions, however, Doug knew more than I. He was a real inspiration.

Doug was also one of the leading musicians in the group. He was the lead guitarist, he sang solos, and he even wrote some songs. But music was not his strongest gift, and he leaned heavily on me for help.

We had a good thing going. He looked to me for musical guidance, and I looked to him for Biblical insight. We learned from one another as we went.

Even after Doug graduated from high school, we continued our relationship for a good number of years. I would be asked to lead the worship and music at conferences, so I would call Doug to bring his guitar and come join me.

Along with several other guys — Tom on the piano, Bill on another guitar, and different people on the electric bass — we had a good team. But it was our rap sessions in the motel rooms that I remember most fondly. We would talk about the Second Coming of Jesus Christ until 2:00 a.m., loving it.

Well, during the years with The Young Folk that followed, new kids came along. They were believers, but most of them didn't have the spiritual maturity of that original group. Doug was no longer there to open the Bible every time there was a desire to know what the Word had to say about something important. Now it was all up to me.

Add to that the fact that the church had never been able to get a viable youth ministry going. I was it. They didn't tell me I would have to be a youth pastor. To this day I don't know how anyone can combine the two roles of youth ministry and ministry of music without feeling schizophrenic. I know some guys tackle it, but my advice to any church or individual considering such a combination is FORGET IT. (I'll probably get some letters for that one.)

Back to The Young Folk. We had some great times with the Scriptures. In fact, we got to the point that we spent 50% of our rehearsal time in spiritual growth activities. What a difference it made. And just as before, I learned more than they did — simply because I had to.

"Harry, what did you think of the sermon today?"

Was this a test? Was there something John wanted me to say? Was there instead something that John wanted to say?

I also wondered whether he was asking me about the content of the sermon or about the way it was delivered. There is certainly a big difference in those two questions, but most people critique the delivery rather than the content.

"What aspect of the sermon are you asking me about, John?"

"Was wondering what you thought when the pastor said that part about tithing. I don't know whether I agree with that or not. Well, I know that God says tithe, but it's not clear to me what that means. Should we tithe the gross income or the net income? Should we give all our tithe to the church, or can we spread it around?

The pastor had made some very pointed comments about all of those particulars. John was disagreeing. He was feeling guilty about it. He was looking for someone on the staff who would agree with him. He obviously hoped that I would be his ally.

Had I not studied the Word of God on that subject on my own, and had I not already wrestled with what I believe are the answers, I would not have known what to say to John. He was one of hundreds of examples of people coming to me to discuss the contents of a sermon. It's a frequent occurrence on the church staff; it's a weekly point of conversation. You need to be Biblically literate to participate.

Some Solutions

Inch by Inch
Daily, systematic Bible study will build a strong foundation.

IT TAKES DISCIPLINE TO LEARN A NEW LANGUAGE. It takes consistent practice to play Bach. It takes skilled coaching to sing with proper resonance support. All that is also true of becoming Biblically literate.

You need to set aside some time in your day for studying the Word. It may be only five minutes, but you need to have a routine.

It takes time to climb a mountain, but the view at the top is marvelous. Tackling the Bible is very similar. As you are digging through one passage, trying to understand it and apply it to your life, it's easy to allow your mind to wander. When mine does, it usually starts asking the question, "If it's going to take me this long and this much effort to get through just this paragraph, how in the world do I expect to get through this whole book?"

That's when I remember one very hot summer when I painted the outside of my house. Yuk. It took all day, every day, for two weeks for me to finish. You know how I got through it? I kept saying over and over a phrase that I had heard Robert Schuller use: "Inch by inch, anything's a cinch."

Remember that. The next time you are trying to teach those thick-headed basses how to sing those sixteenth notes cleanly, take it a note at a time. That's the way with the Bible as well.

Studying the Word of God on your own takes some assistance. You should invest in several good study aids, several different translations, and possibly some good cassette tapes by great Bible teachers.

You should have at least three translations of the Word. It's fun to compare them. There are some publications that contain several translations within the same volume with the texts side by side. Those are very helpful.

If you are intimidated by the Bible, you might want to look at *The Living Bible* or *Good News for Modern Man*. Those editions make it easier to understand. But be aware of the fact that *The Living Bible* is not a translation of the original text — it's a paraphrase of other English translations. For personal devotion, it's great; for accuracy of meaning, it's not always reliable.

Besides various translations, you should get one or two good commentaries on the Bible. Your Christian Bookstore will guide you. The commentaries give scholarly opinions on what certain passages are saying. Notice the use of the word "opinions." Commentaries are great, but they are not to be a substitute for your doing your own digging as to what the Lord meant by the text before you.

I Would Need To Be A Bible Scholar.

A good Bible Dictionary is also a must. Before you study a particular book, read what the writer has to say about it in the Bible Dictionary. When you are dealing with a particular Biblical character or a location, look up the name in the Bible Dictionary. It's very enlightening, and it has the added benefit of not taking up too much time.

If this is new to you, I recommend that you start with one of the Gospels. I chose Matthew; you might prefer John or Mark or Luke. It really doesn't matter: You just need to have a firm grasp on the life and teachings of Jesus.

Then move to an epistle of Paul. I chose Colossians because it is short. See how spiritual I am?

There are two mistakes that I want to encourage you to avoid. One of them is the desire some new Bible students have of jumping into the book of Revelation. Yes, it's intriguing, to say the least. But nobody really understands that book. There are many who will tell you that they have unlocked its secrets. They are on the long list of those who have opinions. If you try to wade through Revelation too soon, you may close the Bible in total frustration.

The second mistake is that many people overlook the need to study the Old Testament. You cannot fully understand the New Testament unless you also understand the Old Testament.

One more thing. I'm convinced that one of the primary reasons God allowed man to invent the cassette tape deck for automobiles is so that we can listen to good teaching tapes while we drive along. If you have not yet discovered what a blessing that is, take the hint.

From Genesis to Maps
Plan time in your schedule for special group Bible studies.

I mentioned The Bethel Series earlier. This two-year course is designed to take you through the entire Bible. After you've had the experience, you have a much greater grasp of the main themes of the Scriptures. You will clearly understand the relationship between the two testaments. It's one of the finest programs I know of its type.

If you have the opportunity to take this course, do so. If your church would like to consider offering this program, you may contact the responsible people for information. Write to:

The Bethel Series
Adult Christian Education Foundation
312 Wisconsin Avenue
Madison, WI 53703

There are other ways to become introduced to the themes of the Bible, such as the Walk Through the Bible program, which is a one-day adventure. All such opportunities will serve you well.

But outside of private, personal Bible study, there is no better way to grow in this area than to join or start a small group that meets at the church or in homes on a regular basis to study the Word together. Small groups offer you an opportunity to ask questions and dialogue your study.

Warning: It isn't all that helpful for a group to come together for Bible study and just share ignorance. You will need a teacher. If you don't have a qualified teacher, perhaps you should train yourself for that role. You will learn more than the students — I promise you!

There are also wonderful helps available in the form of audio and video cassettes. Among the best are those offered by Ligonier Ministries, founded and headed by Dr. R.C. Sproul. They will gladly share information with you on their offerings if you contact them as follows:

Ligonier Ministries
P.O. Box 7500
Orlando, FL 32854-9989
(305) 834-1633

Bring Forth the Royal Diadem
Systematically study and understand your hymn and anthem texts.

One of the most marvelous aspects of being a choir director or choir member is the opportunity to deal with great texts.

Please notice the word I used — texts. There has been a growing tendency to refer to the words of anthems, solos, and larger works as "lyrics." By the dictionary, the word "lyrics" is no problem; but the word is so associated with secular music that it bothers me to use it of an anthem written to worship God. The word "text" has more dignity for me.

I Would Need To Be A Bible Scholar.

You may not agree with that little side trip, but I feel better having pointed it out.

Regardless of what you call the words your choir sings, you need to study them and understand them. Don't take them for granted.

One of the best places for you to prepare for the task of conducting your choir is in your favorite easy chair at home. Take your music there with you, of course. Now without a piano or a tape playing in your ear, open the music. READ THE WORDS. What do they mean? What do they intend to convey? Think of ways that you can make those words jump off of the page for each singer in your choir. Refresh yourself with our English vocabulary and become comfortable with the theology contained in the texts.

You will also make healthy decisions about tempos, phrasing, dynamics, and all of the other interpretive choices you face with the music if you hear it in your mind sitting in that easy chair. Try it and see.

Keep good files and notes on the word studies you do. That's especially true, of course, of the theological studies. If you study the Sermon on the Mount, for instance, you should have a file on it. Your notes should be so clear that were you asked to come teach a class on Matthew 5-7 this week, you could do so.

The time will come when the choir will once again be singing The Beatitudes, or The Lord's Prayer, or "Seek Ye First the Kingdom of God." You will remember that at one point in time you had a good grasp of the meaning of those words, and you even had some great illustrations that helped them take deep roots in your spirit. But just what were they? Let's see... hmmm... can't remember now. Oh well, too bad.

Too bad, indeed. You won't be able to remember all the things you study in the Word of God any more than you can remember all the proofs you used to know in Geometry. So having good notes, well filed and labeled, will be invaluable to you as you prepare for a choir rehearsal.

Speaking of word studies in the Bible, there are some great computer software programs available today containing the entire Bible. Believe it or not, you can type a word or phrase on the screen of your computer and ask it to list all the references for that word/phrase to be found in the entire Bible. It will do so in two seconds — literally! Then you can print out that list or show on the screen and print out the full contents of those verses. If you like, you can ask to see a particular verse in context. Then you can transport whatever you've called up into any other document you are working on with your word processor. Amazing world we live in. The computer age is here to stay, and you should take full advantage of it.

Quick. What Is Your Telephone Number?
Discipline yourself to memorize the Word of God.

If you are asked for your telephone number, you could spout it out right away. Same is true of your address and other statistics like your wife's birthday, the names of your closest living relatives, and perhaps your social security number as well.

Memorization is something we do every day. Memorization is the way most of us got through school.

But how many of us ever take the time and effort to memorize verses of the Bible? It's not difficult. It just takes a little consistent effort.

I love those words in Psalm 119, verses 9 and 11, which say...

> How can a young man keep his way pure? By living
> according to your word.
> I have hidden your word in my heart that I might not
> sin against you.

Hiding the Word of God in our hearts — memorizing the Scriptures — is one of the most rewarding exercises for self improvement I know. And most importantly, it draws you closer to the Father.

There is a hair-raising story told by a man who was in a catastrophic plane accident. It seems that the planes were fogbound at the airport on a small island. Since the terminal was so small, the passengers of many different airlines were sitting in the planes waiting for the fog to lift so that they could take off.

It was a long, long, wait; but the time finally came, and the green light was given. His plane began to taxi out on the runway.

But another pilot, eager to get his flight under way, didn't wait for the proper signal. He decided to take off using another runway.

The two planes collided on the ground. The one that was preparing for flight was sliced in two by the one taking off. Screams were heard everywhere, and jet fuel began to spray all over the cabin and onto the

I Would Need To Be A Bible Scholar.

passengers. Fire broke out. This man reports that people on all four sides of him were in flames and dying. It was a horrifying moment.

There was no time to think. He started running and leaping like a gazelle over the seats of that plane. He saw a hole in the roof of the cabin. To this day, he doesn't know how he had the ability to get through that hole in the ceiling of this huge 747, or how he managed to get to the wing or jump to the ground. He survived with only a sprained ankle. His friend and traveling companion perished, as did hundreds of others.

But the thing that stands out most in his memory were the sounds of the dying and the words that came from his own lips. All around him, people in flames were screaming their curses. Profanity split the air, and the Lord's name was taken in vain over and over.

He reports that he said the first thing that came to his mind. At the top of his lungs he shouted, "Jesus! Jesus! I stand on Your Word!"

He suddenly remembered a Scripture that he had memorized years earlier — Isaiah 43:1-2.

> Fear not, for I have redeemed you:
> I have summoned you by name; you are mine...
> When you walk through the fire, you will not be burned;
> the flames will not set you ablaze.

Hallelujah! The Living Word of God again proved true! This man was miraculously spared.

But he said as he shared this remarkable story that had he not placed the Word of God in his heart, had he not placed Jesus Christ in the front of his mind as his Savior and Lord, he wonders what would have come from his lips. Would he have been like one of those who shouted profanity? Would he have cursed God as he was dying?

He pointed out that when the little black box is recovered from fatal plane crashes, the last words uttered by pilots are often curses to God.

It's a staggering thought and very sobering.

> As water reflects a face,
> so a man's heart reflects the man.
>
> Proverbs 27:19

> For out of the overflow of his heart
> his mouth speaks.
>
> Luke 6:45

Let's hide the Word of God in our hearts. Let's be transformed by the renewal of our minds before the Lord.

Realizing this need, I had The Young Folk go through The Navigators Topical Scriptural Memorization Course. It's a fabulous program that has taken about 60 verses from all over the Bible and placed them in a logical outline by categories such as "Living the New Life" and "Be Christ's Disciple."

Boy did those kids rebel. The most common complaint I heard was, "I have to do this sort of thing in school all day. I don't want to come to church and have to memorize some more!" Typical of our human natures. They didn't have to tell me that people are lazy.

But I forced them to complete the program over the course of the school year. Two verses a week — inch by inch.

You know what? For years and years since that time I have received letters and personal contacts from those young people in which they repeat that the singularly most important and helpful thing they had ever experienced was that Scriptural memorization program. It has really done my heart good.

You should do this for yourself. You should do this for and with your choir. Believe me, many of them will rebel. That's natural. It started in the Garden of Eden. Don't let that stop you. Be persistent and help your brothers and sisters in the Lord commit to memory the important, life-changing text of the Bible itself.

You may write to The Navigators for more information about their particular Scripture memorization course I mentioned as well as some of their other very fine helps. Write to...

The Navigators
P.O. Box 6000
Colorado Springs, CO 80934
(719) 598-1212

One of the best ways to memorize the Word of God is to sing it. In fact, point out to yourself and to your choir that there is already an abundance of the Word up there between those two ears. Just recall the Scriptures that are sung in hymns, anthems, and especially in worship songs.

I've heard report after report, testimony after testimony from choir members and others who say that when they were in moments of deep distress, it was the words of memorized music that brought them comfort and composure. This is a common phenomenon for people preparing to go into surgery. It's often reported by a parent who is rushing their child to the emergency room of the hospital. It's a common story shared by those finding themselves in automobile accidents or other traumatic circumstances. And believe me, it helps when you're sitting in the dentist's chair, too!

Shalom, Shalom
The Word of God best comes to life through a pilgrimage to The Holy Land.

Jack was a travel agent in our congregation. The Lord had laid it upon his heart to give each member of our church staff and spouse a free pilgrimage to The Holy Land.

One by one we made that journey. My opportunity came in 1979. Elizabeth and I enjoyed what for me must be marked as one of the most significant experiences of my life. I seriously sat down a few years ago and tried to list the top ten events of my life. Meeting the Lord, marrying Elizabeth, having our children — those kinds of events are the first to come to everyone's mind. But in that list I also included that first pilgrimage to Israel.

I say first because I have now been back a number of times. As the director of The National Christian Choir in Washington, DC, I had the privilege of taking them to The Holy Land at the invitation of the Government of Israel to be the featured choir in Manger Square in Bethlehem on Christmas Eve. That's something to tell the grandchildren about!

Now I lead tours to The Holy Land as often as I can. Every time I go, I see new things and learn new things. The people that I've had the privilege of taking on this life-changing journey agree with me that there is no experience that parallels it for helping the Word of God come to life.

Come to the Holy Land. Walk in the footsteps of Jesus Christ. See the Old Testament and the New Testament side by side. Hear the sounds, see the holy places, eat the food, hear the music, watch the dancing, worship with other believers in the places where it all took place.

I believe in this experience so much that I never tire of telling other Christians that they need to make this a priority in their life. If you aren't sure that this is something you really want to do, then approach it from an attitude of obedience. Go to Jerusalem, go to the Sea of Galilee, and discover that what I'm saying is true.

Taking your choir on tour will cause them to develop as a family. It doesn't matter much where you take them — touring together and ministering through music together is a fun, inspiring, enlightening, growth-filled time.

But taking your choir on a singing pilgrimage to The Holy Land is an unbeatable combination. You will be equipping them in so many ways that you won't believe the positive results.

Later, as you sing Psalms, hymns, and spiritual songs, you will "see" in your mind's eye what you are singing about. You will be amazed at how often the anthems you sing will bring you once again to the memory of that educational pilgrimage. The same will happen as you hear sermons and teachings — and especially as you read the Word.

Yes, you need to be a Biblical scholar — as least Biblically literate — to lead the choir. There's no better way to do that than to visit the Land of the Bible and see where it all began.

Get in touch with me. Let's go to Israel together!!

CHAPTER 7

THEY DIDN'T TELL ME

◆ ◆ ◆

I Would Have To Be A Servant.

The Situation

THE SUMMER TOUR WAS APPROACHING, and there were about two dozen teen-agers who could not afford the trip. We never left anyone behind because of money, so we were gearing up for our annual fund-raisers.

What will it be this year? Shall we auction off an evening at the city's finest gourmet restaurant? Or perhaps we could have home-a-rama in the fashionable part of town. If only we had thought to breed minks during the year, perhaps we could have taken care of our financial problems in short order.

Well, since none of those ideas took wings, we had to come up with something new and exciting. I know — let's have a car wash!

What a novel idea! Lots of people drive cars and get them dirty. Perhaps they would like to bring their dirty cars to the church parking lot some Saturday in the spring and get the winter crud off of their vehicles.

Now who would have thought of that — a car wash?

As I think back to my days of analyzing Gregorian Chant, and when I remember how it felt to don my rented tuxedo to conduct the choir and orchestra for Handel's "Chandos Anthems," it just doesn't seem possible that I would be called upon to scrounge for rags, plastic buckets, rags, paper towels, glass cleaner, rags, soap, and — oh yes — rags.

Well, I did. For a donation of $2.00 or more, you could get just enough soap film on your car windshield to know you had been to The Young Folk's annual car wash.

You know what never occurred to me in making the plans? Where would we get the hoses and water? Thank goodness for our church administrator who had thought of that for me and supplied both the hoses and the key to the outdoor water faucet. Otherwise those 60 teen-agers would have had nothing with which to wash the soap off of one another. At least the kids got clean!

Oh, did I mention that we added a bake sale to the car wash idea? Really worked great, if I could keep myself from eating all the profit.

They didn't tell me that I would have to run a car wash with calories.

***

Carl had a youth choir, too. His was in the Northeast in a large, non-denominational church. His choir also went on summer tour, to the beach twice during the months of June through August, down to a Fun in the Sun experience in Georgia in August, and to a Young Life camp in New York in July.

His choir also sang in churches around their city. They didn't get around as often as mine, but probably about six times a year they would set out for The First Church of the Unknown.

Carl's problem, however, is that someone at the church thought it would be a good idea to buy a bus. Not a lovely new bus, mind you. Not one with air conditioning and a rest room in the back. Nope. This was a real winner of an antique. It was of the Chitty-Chitty Bang-Bang variety.

And guess who was elected by the wise old elders of the church to be the driver? You guessed it — Carl.

I Would Have To Be A Servant.

Had he ever driven a bus before? Carl had never even driven a van, much less a vehicle 14 times that big!

Did the engine work? Yes, on Tuesday afternoons from 2:15 until around 4:00. Was Carl a mechanic? Yes, if that meant taking your car to Sears for an oil change.

The poor guy had to get a special license to have this rare privilege, and he was allowed to pay for it out of his own pocket. Such generous wise old elders.

Nobody ever told Carl that he would have to be a chauffeur.

***

My choir room had built-in risers. On those risers I had those awful gray metal folding chairs that someone has christened the state of the art for churches. I had a large choir, so I had to have a large number of chairs. There were over 100, in fact. Count 'em. 1, 2, 3, 4...

The choir room was used by the adult choir for whom it was designed. No problem. But it was also used by the children's choirs, the handbell players, the teen-age choir, and several Bible study groups during the week in the Christian Lay Academy. Worst of all, on Tuesday afternoons, it was used by the rock-roaring, terror-slinging junior highs. All 100 of them descended on that room like killer bees.

After everyone used that room — especially those delightful 7th and 8th graders — the chairs were a mess. It sometimes looked like somebody brought in a giant egg beater and got lots of tension out of their system with "my" chairs.

So guess who had to go to the choir room before every rehearsal and every Sunday morning and straighten out those awful grey metal folding chairs? You guessed it — my assistant minister of music. Aha. Fooled you. Did you think *I* was going to do that?

Well, in fact, I did — often. My assistant and I both *hated* that mess. So we shared the job. Some day I should ask him if his perception was that we shared it equally. No, on second thought, I think I'll skip it.

Nobody told me that some day I would have to straighten over 100 of those awful gray folding metal chairs. 73, 74, 75, 76, 77...

***

Someone gave my church some absolutely beautiful seven-tiered candelabras. There were two of them — one on each side of the front of the sanctuary. They stood on the floor and were about seven feet tall. They were made of cast iron and overlaid with hand crafted metal of some kind. I think some of it might have been copper and some of it brass.

I Would Have To Be A Servant.

There were seven candles in each. We put tall white candles in them for each Sunday morning service. Then we trained some youngsters to be acolytes. Did I say "we?" I should correct that to "I." I'm amazed we didn't have to call the rescue squad with those acolytes.

Every Sunday morning, before the choir came to rehearse for the first service, I would go to the sanctuary to make sure the chairs were correct in the choir loft and that the organist and I had all our signals straight. But it never failed: As I would walk into the sanctuary, I would discover week after week that someone had put the candelabras several feet off their appointed spots. They wouldn't be balanced on each side. One or more of the candles would be crooked. It bothered me.

So Sunday after Sunday I would go to one side and then the other to straighten the candles and move those monsters into position.

Folks, we're talking pounds! I mean those babies weighed more than my mother-in-law. Physical labor is not my thing, and I certainly don't like the idea of lifting heavy objects just before I have to conduct. But it seemed like if I didn't do this "little" task, it wouldn't get done. So I did.

Did I resent it? Oh no. And if you believe that one, I'll tell you about the time I caught a mermaid off the coast of France.

It was particularly annoying when I would come into the sanctuary on those Sunday mornings and find that the custodians had failed to replace the candles in the holders. It meant that I had to take out the 14 candles, dispose of them, find replacements in the supply closet, put them in their little holes, and then walk around the sanctuary at several angles to make sure they were straight. This all took time. Time was not something I had much of, since the choir would be arriving shortly. I still had to talk to the organist and have one last meeting with the pastor.

After the candles were happy, I had to move the piano. We were blessed with a grand piano. It was heavy, too. I guess I should have lifted weights as a teen-ager, because these obstacles now made me worry about a hernia.

In case you can't tell, they didn't tell me that I would need a moving van before the service could begin.

***

There was yet another task that fell unto moi. This one wasn't heavy, but it was high. Somebody had to change the light bulbs in the choir loft before the service could begin.

Yes, we had a good custodial staff at this church, but those candelabras and the most important light bulbs in the sanctuary had an uncanny way of demanding attention just before the service and when the custodians were off duty.

Those light bulbs were in the ceiling — the high ceiling. How high? Nosebleed high!

This challenge called for a ladder. The ladder was a long way away. It was in a very dirty closet. I was in my suit and tie. But I changed those bulbs anyway.

Is this what they meant by saying that I should be the light of the world?

I Would Have To Be A Servant.

*
* *

During graduate school I took one church job just for the money. God didn't call me to that church — at least not according to my heart; but He did allow me to learn and grow through some bad experiences there as He also provided for me and my wife financially.

I was hired to play the organ as well as direct the choir in that position. I did that combined work for a number of years in a number of different churches, until I wised up. I think those two jobs should be split between two people. I could say lots about that, but let's move on.

The pipe organ there must have been found in an ancient tomb in the hills of Scotland. It was old. It was very, very old.

It wheezed when it should have diapasoned. And it had an entertaining way of playing all by itself during the prayer or the sermon.

Never have I seen an organ with more ciphers. Watch out for the scale of G Major, because every other note in it would stick.

Every Sunday morning I would arrive at Northside, wondering if the instrument would get us through today. Nearly every Sunday I would climb into the organ chamber and pull out pipes that just wouldn't quit play-

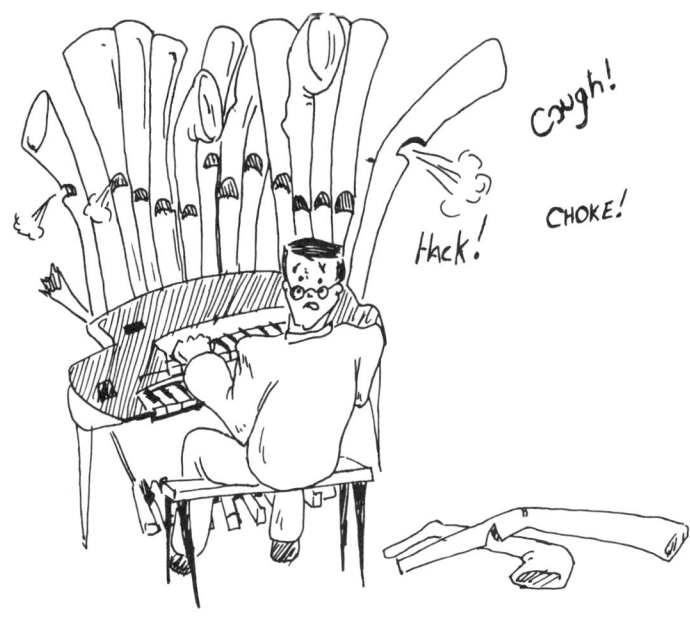

ing unless their air supply was stifled. Have you ever been in an organ chamber? Have you ever been in an ancient tomb Scottish organ chamber? Until you have, don't try to tell me about how much dust there is in the Sahara. Don't mention to me how many spiders there are with the Addams Family.

Now that I think about it, that old ladder closet wasn't all that dirty at all. At least when I left Northside, I moved up in the world.

Well, it happened again. They didn't tell me I would have to be an organ repair man when I grew up.

Some Solutions

IN ADDITION TO SOME PAPER, PENS, paper clips, rubber bands, and a metronome in your office at the church, add these items — paper towels, Windex, Endust, rags, Pine Sol, Super Glue, rags, Ivory Liquid, razor blades, Raid, rags, and rags.

You will undoubtedly find yourself in the role of a servant. You will need a pair of jeans, perhaps some overalls, and the willingness to do a number of things that your ego may try to tease you into thinking are not your job.

Allow time in your Sunday morning schedule for the unexpected. I learned long ago that I needed to get to the church plenty early on Sunday mornings to check on the piano hammers, the thermostat, the hymnals, the bulletins, and lots of other details that were necessary for this thing to get off the ground.

One of my problems was that I did not have a servant heart. I mean I found it more blessed to be served than to serve.

Some people have a gift of serving. You may be one of them. As for me, I have that gift, too; only it's thimble size, not tumbler.

Attitude makes the difference. If you take the attitude that I often found myself taking, you will probably do those necessary things, but you will resent it. You will grumble. And nobody likes a grumble bee.

Before you get too old, get some experience driving a van. Then try a truck or a bus. You just may need it.

Learn how to organize car washes and bake sales. It's easy, actually. I don't need to detail it here. But you have to make the decision that you will indeed learn how to organize.

Get to know the supply closet at your church. Does the church own a ladder? Will it take more than one guy to handle it? Where are the light bulbs? Knowing those kinds of details in advance is much like having a flashlight handy just in case the electricity fails. That reminds me — find the fuse box and the replacement fuses, too.

One of the areas in which you should definitely get some training is the care and maintenance of pianos. Find a good piano tuner. If he's really good, he will probably call himself a piano technician. Ask him to talk you through the mechanism of the instrument. Have him show you how to take it apart and put it back together again. What do you do if the damper pedal isn't working? He'll show you. What happens if a hammer starts striking two different strings at once? He'll walk you through that, too.

The same is true of the pipe organ, but that's a lot more sensitive. You are better off leaving the tricky things to the experts in that department. But at least you ought to get friendly with the spiders in the organ chamber occasionally.

Keep a good spirit about you. Serving where needed and helping get things done can be rather fulfilling, you know.

Remember what Jesus said in Mark 10:43-44? "Whoever wants to become great among you must be your servant, and whoever wants to be first must be slave of all."

By the way, don't forget that your old worn out tee shirt makes a great rag.

CHAPTER 8

THEY DIDN'T TELL ME

◆ ◆ ◆

I Would Have To Be An Administrator.

The Situation

JUST TWO MILES FROM CAMPUS and across the railroad tracks was the red brick building that housed the church I served during my undergraduate years of college. For just a small community, this church had a decent membership of around 500 worshipers and a fun choir of 20-25. At Christmas time, we could count on nearly 50.

One of the things that this church lacked, however, was a decent music library. All of the people who had come before me just kept recycling the old music that was already there. I don't know how those choir members (or the congregation for that matter) stood it all those years. I mean, just how many times can you sing Stainer's "God So Loved the World" and stay awake?

Oops. Perhaps I'd better quickly add that I really love that old piece. I'm just pointing out the obvious — constantly repeating any music is boring.

So I saw it as my duty — my privilege, actually — to change the situation. There was a lady (I use the term loosely) who ran the show. There was no music committee, just the music chairman. In those days we didn't have to say chairperson. But she was it.

She agreed with me, thank goodness, and got the church to grant me a modestly adequate budget with which to purchase new music.

That was the first time in my life that I had the responsibility of going shopping for the music the choir would sing. It was exhilarating.

Now let's see, what music should I buy? The first thought that came to me was to go back to my high school days and pick some of the anthems that I had most enjoyed from my former church. That was easy and only took a few phone calls to get the information. But in a matter of a few months, that easy street was well traveled.

Just where does one find new music? Pretty important question for a choir director to answer. I was soon scrambling for information on music review services and the like. Before too very long, I was receiving new releases in the mail. Wonderful.

But nobody told me that there were so many of them! Week after week I received packets of music from various publishers and review services. I was a full-time student, remember? I had to study for my classes, so I would just have to put those new releases in a pile until I could get the time to play through them.

Well, the pile grew. Soon there were two piles. I can remember having to find some boxes to put those piles into so that I could carry all that music to the practice room at nights to play through it. This was becoming a burden.

The next step was to find a dumpster where I could pitch all the garbage that the publishers were sending me. Out of each hundred titles, I felt euphoric if I could find just one good one.

The next question that plagued me was where to go to purchase the one-in-a-hundred winner. "Easy," said the secretary of the music department at school. "Go where we go. There's a music store in the city that has a great selection, or they can get you anything you want."

She was experienced, so I didn't question her recommendation. Besides, it was a local call.

That was the beginning of a long road to frustration. Yes, they could get anything I wanted for the choir, but she didn't tell me that Easter might come and go before the music arrived. I had to change my plans at the eleventh hour many a month. I also paid full price for that kind of service.

Since those early days I have learned that there is service and then there is service. Finding the right music distributor, the one that gives great service, is just about as important as knowing where to find the men's room after three cups of coffee.

I also learned years later that paying retail isn't necessary. But at first, anyway, nobody told me that selecting and buying music was going to be such a challenge.

I Would Have To Be An Administrator.

Patricia was the first full-time minister of music that her church had ever hired. The church was located on one of the Great Lakes in sight of the water. I enjoyed visiting there twice and got to see some fascinating scenery.

But that's not the point of this story. Patricia ran into a universal problem when she took the job, and it fell upon her shoulders to do something about it.

You see, her predecessors had purchased plenty of anthems, collections, and not a few cantatas. But they were just stacked on shelves, in boxes, and in filing cabinet drawers.

Matilda was the "choir librarian." I would have hated to see that lady's kitchen. Her sense of organization was a monstrosity. But did she know where everything was to be found? You bet. "Now let's see, I put that one... isn't that the one that has something in it about sparrows?... I put it in the box on the shelf in the closet behind the organ. But that other one you want, the one that has the real high notes for the sopranos, I believe it's at home. Just wasn't a good place for it here."

"How many others do you have at home, Matilda?"

"Oh, I don't know. 40 or 50, I guess." Patricia reported that Matilda had an annoying way of giggling when she said things like that.

Patricia had a few things to resolve here. First she had to gather all the church's music into one location, and that location needed to be the church itself. Then she had to figure out how she was going to organize that music so that she would be able to find it without Matilda. Then she had the hard part to deal with: She had to keep Matilda from becoming hurt that her methods of organization were being replaced by more sane techniques.

Nobody had warned Patricia that she would have to be a music librarian. But she figured it out.

***

Choir rehearsals have a way of becoming chaotic. People arriving with coats and laughter, music to be distributed, information to be shared, choir clowns sharing their latest jokes, singing, talking while you're talking, planning, praying, and of course dismissal.

If you are not the captain of this ship, then your rehearsal has the strong potential of either going aground or meeting a watery grave before its time.

Sandy is a female. She is the minister of music of a medium-sized church in Atlanta. Philip is a tenor in her choir. Philip doesn't like female choir directors. Philip is also the choir clown, so he loves to make jokes about female choir directors to all the other tenors who will listen.

Sandy is fighting a losing battle in choir rehearsals with Philip and all his chauvinistic buddies. It's very sad, because Sandy is one of the more gifted, creative ministers of music I've encountered.

Nobody told Sandy that she might not be accepted by some narrow-minded choir members just because she's a woman. It's true.

Nobody told me that leading a choir rehearsal could be tough. I thought everyone who came to choir would love the music, love me, love the routines, love discipline, and love the Lord. Surprise.

***

Horace is the choir director of a large church in North Carolina with an exciting, growing music program. His is one of those locations where the pastor just might become threatened because Horace is doing such a superb job.

Horace has a choir for just about every grade level through school, numerous handbell choirs, a growing church orchestra, an adult choir of nearly 100 voices, a singing Christmas Tree each December, and loads of potential for burnout.

Horace has an organist and a very sizable music budget. But much to my amazement, Horace is not granted secretarial support from the church's budget. With a program the size of his, Horace ought to have not only a full-time secretary, but he could use a full-time paid assistant as well.

I had lunch with Horace after a conference I was doing, and I asked him how in the world he managed to administrate such a large circus.

"Volunteers," was his immediate response. "I couldn't do it without a large number of volunteers."

I nodded my head with understanding. I already suspected that I knew the answer to the next question I was to ask him. Here goes.

"Well what do you consider your greatest headache, your most annoying problem in this program, Horace?"

"That's easy — it's those volunteers!"

I Would Have To Be An Administrator.

Bingo. I was right. Anyone who has ever been in the position of having to recruit and oversee volunteers in the ministry or any other activity will tell you that it is often easier just to do it yourself.

Volunteers are wonderful when they do their thing. The problem is that almost all volunteers let you down along the way. If you find a good volunteer who is reliable, consistent, loyal, and faithful to the task, give them an eagle badge and treat them very, very nicely. You are blessed.

Churches thrive on volunteers. Your music ministry will definitely need to get in step. But don't be surprised when the burden of following up on those volunteers falls on your shoulders and your schedule.

"Harry, what do you think about having a nursery during choir rehearsal?"

That question has come to me at just about every job I've had. It's a great service to the young couples in the choir with babies. Where I live, teen-aged baby-sitters charge enough to need a Form 1040 each April. So offering a nursery at your church for choir rehearsal can actually enable those parents to attend. They'd go broke otherwise.

But nobody told me I would have to manage a nursery. That's right. If you have child care during your rehearsals or other choir events, you will probably inherit the responsibility for it.

This is one of those areas where you will have to manage volunteers carefully, because dealing with little ones is a very serious undertaking.

You know who my greatest problems have come from in this area? It's the day care center of the church or the Sunday school nursery people who have given me the most grief. Those people who are responsible for the church's nursery all the time are very protective of their space and their equipment. They have to be: They must meet certain standards of safety and cleanliness as required by law that allow them to operate. And it seems that any time we have wanted to use their facilities for the babies of our choir members, they have come after me with complaints.

I wasn't prepared for this one. But along the way I have learned that the nursery is no place to fool around.

***

Things really began to go well for me and the church I served in Cincinnati. So many people were coming to the two morning worship services that it was standing room only. The choir grew to 125 voices with a waiting list that was sometimes five years long. Sunday school space was at a premium, and offices were being created in every corner imaginable.

Sounds great from the outside looking in; but believe me, these problems produced inconvenience, chaos, trauma, and acid indigestion.

For the choir of 125 voices, I had a choir loft that sat 75. People had to literally volunteer to sit on the floor in the hall adjacent to the choir loft during the services.

Due to lack of air conditioning, the choir rehearsal room became a steam bath after the first half hour of rehearsal. And you should have talked to the brides who fainted from the heat in the sanctuary during summer weddings.

Dust and humidity played havoc with the pipe organ and pianos. We would plan organ and piano duets on many Sunday mornings only to discover just before the service that they were not in tune with one another.

Sectional rehearsals were fun. Tenors, you go into my office. Basses, why don't you look for space in the men's room. Altos, how do you like closets?

The offices were nice, but I didn't need an intercom between my office and the two on either side of me. It's a good thing that the pastor to my left liked music, because he had to contend with my piano and stereo every day. As for me, I found his counseling sessions very interesting.

As for storage, that was no problem: There wasn't any.

You never know what your facilities will be like, and you never know if or when you might outgrow them. Don't be surprised if you find yourself in the business of managing space.

Robert is the minister of music of a rapidly growing church in Kansas City. He is currently facing similar problems to the ones I've just described, and he called me to talk about it. He remembers visiting me at my church in Cincinnati years ago and seeing the space problem first hand. Now that he is in the same predicament, he wants to grumble a bit.

But Robert can see a light at the end of the tunnel. His church has voted to build, and Robert is being asked to do research and make recommendations. Not only is he responsible for helping the proper committees design an ideal worship environment, but he also has the privilege of helping design the new music wing. He's looking forward to a rehearsal room that mirrors the choir loft, practice rooms, sectional rehearsal rooms, offices, greatly increased storage space, and even a recording studio of sorts built right into the complex.

Has Robert ever done anything like this before? Nope. What does he know about lighting, air circulation, ceiling height, riser lift, people movement, acoustical properties of various building materials? Robert has an enviable opportunity, but a formidable challenge. How much time is this all taking him? Don't ask!

There's a question echoing in my memory. It's been posed to me so many times that I ought not be surprised when it comes up again. And I've talked with innumerable others in the ministry who have encountered the same mind set.

What is the question? It's this: "What do you do with your time?"

Just thinking about it at this moment brings back the memories of "You've got to be kidding!" My wife didn't see me. My kids wondered who this man was who was coming home to eat and then leaving again. My doctor was telling me to slow down and take a trip to Florida (which I couldn't afford, by the way). And these dodos on the Administrative Committee wanted to know what I did to justify my salary.

To be fair with them, they had a job to do. Their responsibility was to monitor the staff's work so that they could give feedback both pro and con. They decided who got raises and how much, so job evaluation was the normal process.

Regardless of how fair it was, however, I couldn't help feeling a little insulted each time the question came up. Have you ever felt that way?

For me it was not just the fact that I had to defend myself that way, but it was the way in which some of those guys would ask the question. There was a sideways glance, a tensing of the eyes, a somber tone in the voice that reminded me of my father's asking, "Where have you been in the car tonight?"

Being a minister of music is not a nine-to-five job. If you think it is, you're in Fantasy Land. That does not necessarily mean, however, that you always have to start work *before* nine, or that you will go home *after* five. No, there are many days when you have the luxury of coming in mid morning or going home early. If it weren't for some of that flexibility, you'd have to have a cot in your office and a toothbrush in your desk drawer.

But when one of those administrative types asks, "How many hours did you spend on the job during the last three months?", he really wants to know. And you'd better be prepared to figure it out.

There are countless details associated with organizing a music program, but lots of choir directors forget that includes organizing yourself, too.

Some Solutions

GET OUT YOUR CALENDARS, your graph paper, your pencils, and your thinking cap. You are now an administrator, whether you want to be one or not.

The Bible tells us that one of the gifts of the Holy Spirit is the gift of administration. Please, Lord, shower us with that gift!

This One Is Good For the Choir with No Tenors
Finding new music for your choir takes a significant commitment of time.

To keep a choir fresh and vital, you need to offer them new musical selections to sing regularly. That is not the only way to keep them fresh and vital, of course, but it is definitely high on the list.

How much new music should you purchase? That answer varies widely with philosophies and music budgets. I've already said that I believe 75% of the music should be new music, but that's very subjective. I've heard others say half, while I've also heard the idea that one piece a month is sufficient.

You have to decide for yourself how to tackle that question. Once you've arrived at a percentage, however, you have to go through that budget request process we talked about so that you will be able to afford your decision.

Just where do you find that new music for your choir to sing? There are many sources, and you should avail yourself of a large variety of them.

No one source is going to give you the variety you need. No one source is going to expose you to the countless gems out there that are just right for your choir.

There are numerous denominational publication houses that seek to keep their constituents informed of new music releases. One of the largest and most helpful is through the Southern Baptist denomination. Their large variety of resources are geared to both stylistic differences as well as ability.

The Methodist church has done a fine job in this area as well; but like the Baptist church, I find a certain predictability of style in these resources. Not that you shouldn't tap them — you definitely should. But keep looking.

When I first started working in that church just across the railroad tracks back in college, I needed new resources. So I did what my music professor told me to do. I wrote letters to about a dozen different music publishers and asked them if they would put me on their list to receive new releases.

Many of them did. Several others wrote back and said that they had a choral music review service. For a modest fee, they would put me on their list, and all my music buying needs would be solved.

Those clubs proved to be good, but once again I found myself locked into receiving lots of material in similar styles. After all, Augsburg is Augsburg, Schirmer is Schirmer, and Lillenas is Lillenas. There are many, many different music publishers, and all of them have something interesting to offer.

We at MUSIC REVELATION offer our own Music Review Club. If you'll excuse a blatant commercial for a few moments, we want to make sure you know about it. Every month we mail out a packet of highly-selective anthems that we choose from among the new releases of over 50 different publishers. We also take the time to write out some rehearsal and performance ideas for each title to try and help you get the most out of the music.

We've had some very fine feedback about the job we do in trying to pick music that really works and music that reaches all sizes of congregations with all kinds of stylistic preferences. It's the only club of its type that we know of, and it's very reasonable. It will save you tons of time. At the back of this book is more information on how you can avail yourself of this opportunity to find the best in new music for your choir.

Now let's get back to our discussion.

With the pursuit of variety comes an avalanche of music. Pile builds on top of pile, and the amount of time required to play through each piece is tremendous.

I Would Have To Be An Administrator.

I tried to keep up with the influx on a regular basis. That's like the person who has quit smoking — a thousand times. Every promise I made to myself to attack that stack went the way of the wind. Every time more music arrived in the mail, I found myself groaning.

I finally devised a plan for myself that worked for me. It's certainly adaptable, but it's worth considering.

Once a year I set aside one week to do nothing but read through music. It was always the week following Easter for me. That particular week was one when I would give the choir a holiday from regular weekly rehearsals. They always put in extra efforts during Holy Week, singing three services on Easter Day itself. That little vacation was much needed for them.

For several of those years, my wife would take our two small children on a trip to visit grandmother. I had the house to myself, and that was ideal.

From morning until bedtime, I played through music. My eyes would rotate in their sockets occasionally, and everything would begin to sound the same sometimes; but that concentrated effort was just right for me. I took great joy in knowing that I had a specific time set aside to devour that mountain of music, and I took even greater joy in seeing it disappear.

Whenever I found a piece that I really liked, I would put it into a folder. The name of that folder was "Consider." During the year to follow, I would grab that folder and review its contents for pieces that I might be interested in doing. It might be several years before a title found its way out of that folder and into the choir's hands, because I would only choose it when I thought it was right for the time or perfect for coordination with an upcoming sermon.

There was another folder, however. This one was labeled "Definite." These were the pieces that gave me chill bumps when I played through them the first time. On the front of those titles I would put a check mark. That was my seal of approval. But then if I was ready to stand up and cheer about an anthem, it received a check mark *and* an asterisk. Those were obviously my favorites of all.

Those two folders were priceless possessions for me. They stood in a little holder right beside the piano in my office at the church. They were my security blanket in planning the music for the future, and I always knew that right at my finger tips I had music that ministered.

While playing through all that new music was a fun challenge, and while I became exposed to plenty of good material in the process, there was still another method of proven worth — one that has emerged as the most popular for most ministers of music. That, of course, is the choral music reading session.

All over the country at many different times of the year, publishers and music distributors host choral music reading workshops. Choir directors from the region gather in a large banquet room at a hotel or in a church sanctuary, for instance, and sing through the new releases on display for that day. It's a great way to hear how the pieces will work for you, and it keeps your sight-reading ability sharpened. You meet new people and rekindle old aquaintances. You often meet some composers and publishers face to face, getting a better idea of their personalities and their thoughts behind the music they offer.

Of course, going to one of these reading sessions takes stamina. Just like playing through 5,000 tunes, singing them all day long has an hypnotic effect as well.

Look around before jumping into these conferences. Some of them also offer some classes or workshops during the day. That's a real bonus, giving you a break from the routine of reading music and giving you an opportunity to grow in some area of your ministry. I guess my biggest complaint about most of these reading sessions is that they don't allow enough time for workshops to suit me. I keep hearing that complaint from the participants as well, but the hosts of these conferences are usually there to sell music. The complaints tend to fall on deaf ears.

Lots of choir directors have discovered the benefits of going to a choral reading session. The problem is that they will often go to the same one over and over. I've been to so many of them that I've discovered the advantage of variety. Going to different parts of the country and meeting new people as you do is one of the growth points that I would like to encourage.

By the way, those new people you meet at these conferences are perhaps one of your best resources for finding new music. When you go, eat lunch or dinner with many different ministers of music. Ask them to share with you their top ten favorite anthems — either of the past year or for all time. Always carry a notebook and pencil with you, and jot down their responses. You could and should cultivate that same type of relationship with other ministers of music in your town. Go to lunch regularly to share music, ideas, highs, lows, and visions. Some of the best choral literature available and some of your best inspirations will come through the recommendation of someone else in your field.

If This Is July, It Must Be Christmas
*Plan ahead and establish a calendar for
your music selections.*

Each fall you need to purchase a desk calendar for the coming year that shows you the year one month at a time. Make sure that it has large squares on it with plenty of space for you to write in.

This is your planning calendar for the Sunday music selections. Using a pencil only, you will write in the titles and composers of each piece you plan to use in the coming months. You might also want to include the music library number, if the piece already has one assigned.

Why do you use pencil? Obviously for flexibility. Just when you thought it was safe to sing about apples, the pastor will announce that his sermon will be on grapefruit. Use a pencil!

How far in advance should you plan? Ideally I would recommend that you look six months into the future at all times. Realistically, you will probably do it a little differently.

For me the routine went like this. In July I would pencil in all the selections for September through December. That's a heavy time of the year, considering all the extra demands of Christmas. In November, I would take care of January through May, covering the end of the school year basically. In April, I would attack the three summer months that were left.

Christmas music in July? Absolutely. I'm amazed at the frantic search for just the right Christmas music that some choir directors subject themselves to in October. That's dumb. You need to be much better organized than that.

Most publishers today release all their new Christmas titles in the spring. At the latest, you should be able to see this year's Advent and Christmas selections no later than June.

But if you keep a "Consider" and a "Definite" file handy, you will probably have seasonal music on tap there for you to draw from at any time of the year. It's not necessary for your choir to sing only brand new copyrights, you know. Sometimes the older things are considerably better than the new ones anyway. So if a piece has been in the "Consider" file for a few years, so what?

There are literally thousands of new choral releases each year. Your job is to look at as many of them as your eyeballs can stand, make your wisest selections, and do it far enough in advance that you will avoid any last-minute panic. Get yourself organized.

File That Under "Inspirational"
A well organized music library is a blessing to you and your successor.

I've poked around enough music libraries in churches to know that far too many of us don't know how to do this right. Putting the latest acquisition into a filing cabinet at the rear of the drawer is not my idea of being creative.

First of all, you must have the music library all in one place and in the church facility. Forget the idea of having it in your home or tucked away in anybody else's basement for that matter. You need to have control over this valuable inventory, and you need access to it at all times.

What if something happens to the well-meaning music librarian who has the only key to her apartment where your music is stored? What if there's a fire there? And what if you need your copies of "The Lord's Prayer" tomorrow night, and she's visiting her aunt in Florida? Get that library where it belongs.

If I could design my music library any way I wanted it, I would have the titles in music file boxes especially designed for that purpose rather than in manila file folders standing in a filing cabinet. Those boxes are sturdy and far more protective of the music than the file folders. The boxes come in various widths so that the music won't curl up the way it might in a filing cabinet. Each box can be easily labeled so that you can read it from a distance, unlike the tab of the traditional manila folder or even an envelope.

By placing the music in the boxes and placing the boxes on shelves, you may move the boxes around more easily than you can rearrange files. The reason is that the filing drawer fills up quickly. When you buy six new anthems, and you want four of them to go into the same drawer to keep them alphabetized, it's a real chore to shift everything around. Moving the boxes on the shelves is much easier.

Where can you get those boxes? There are several great sources, but I'm not going to do any commercials here. Contact me if you get hung up, but I suspect your normal music distributor can supply that information for you easily.

That reminds me, you should get your name on the mailing list for catalogs from several music specialty houses. That's where you find such items as music filing boxes, risers, music stand lights, oversized staff paper, etc. Again, if you can't find any of these, contact me. The information is at the back of this book.

Of the two ways of alphabetizing your music — either by title or by composer's last name — pick the title. For one thing, you are going to remember the title next year before you are going to remember the composer (unless of course you are the composer yourself). Also one of the reasons for establishing a well organized music library is so that your successor can find things easily, too. They'll want to shoot you if you catalog by composer.

Having your music neatly stacked away in a climate-controlled room is great, but you will also need a system for looking up things. You won't always remember the title either. Or perhaps you will remember both the title and the composer's name, but you really want to know whether or not you have enough copies. Or isn't that the anthem that your friend at the church down the street borrowed last year? Did he ever give it back?

At the very least, establish a cross-indexed card file that will give you some quick glances at the contents of your music library. Separate things in that file by voicings, by seasons, by special applications (Communion, Mother's Day, Thanksgiving, etc.), and by Scriptural reference if you feel ambitious enough to do that. That last category, by the way, may turn out to be one of your most treasured.

Best of all, get a computer. The programs available to handle your data base of the music library will greatly simplify your life.

Every choir member should be given a membership number. You're the director, so give yourself #1; give the accompanist #2; then make sure that your Prima Donna is #3.

Whenever you receive a new piece of music, put the numbers corresponding to your choir membership on the face of the music either with a bold marker or with a rubber stamp. I prefer to put those numbers in the upper right corner. Whenever you repeat an anthem, #24 always gets copy #24. When you finish singing a title this week, you will know who to chase if #24 doesn't get returned.

If you catalog your music numerically rather than alphabetically, then the library number should go into the upper left corner of the front cover. Using a different method of noting those two numbers is a good idea (one stamped and the other hand written, for instance). That keeps the choir members from getting confused.

I actually prefer to keep my music library organized numerically rather than alphabetically. It's far easier to add a new box to the empty place on the shelf than it is to try to fit something into a tight space just because it's title starts with "G." There is also a tendency to know that anthems with higher numbers were acquired later, and there will probably be more copies of them as a result.

One of the best things you can do for yourself is to raise up a reliable, competent, volunteer music librarian. He or she can devote all their attention to this whole thing. They can number the music, make out the file cards or enter the data into the computer, sort the music when it is returned, chase the six or seven who never seem to turn in the music when they should, and keep the music repaired when it gets torn and crumpled. When you find that person, take them to lunch regularly and send them flowers: They are a gold mine.

I Want Everybody to Know About My Tupperware Party

Verbal announcements at choir rehearsal eat up valuable time.

The larger your choir, the more announcements the people are going to want to make. The more active your church, the more announcements you will need to make.

Just like in the Sunday morning service, announcements are a necessity. You need to find a way to make sure they are made, but don't let them become the tail wagging the dog.

I Would Have To Be An Administrator.

My solution to that has always been "Choir Notes." For every rehearsal, I type up a sheet of announcements that is then duplicated on the church's copy machine. Each choir member has a slot where his or her music folder and hymnal are kept. Before the rehearsal the music librarian puts "Choir Notes" into each slot.

"Choir Notes" is usually a full page and sometimes even overflows onto side two. This announcement sheet is not just *my* means of communicating with my people, but it is *their* means of communicating with one another.

You see, we don't allow verbal announcements in the choir rehearsal if they can be placed in choir notes. That is a simple procedure that dramatically reduces the time-consuming announcement fever that overcomes many groups. If you want to advertise free kittens, use "Choir Notes." If your daughter is the lead in the school play, use "Choir Notes." It works.

There are some other great uses for this little publication. At the top of the page you may list all the titles you will be singing in the rehearsal that night and the order in which you will be singing them. That's a matter of simple organization that every choir rehearsal should enjoy. You could use a chalk board for the same purpose, but by using "Choir Notes," you force your choir members to pick it up and read it.

That reminds me: I tell my choir members that they are *responsible* for the contents of "Choir Notes" even if they miss rehearsal. Sounds just like school, doesn't it?

In that publication I also list by date the anthems that the choir will be singing each Sunday for the next month. They can always see at a glance what's coming up that way. That gives your choir members some security that they deserve. They like to know that you know what you're doing, and they like to know how much time they have left to master the hard parts of each title.

"Choir Notes" is also useful for printing choir member's birthdays or anniversaries. Everybody likes to be remembered for their birthday from time to time. Of course that means you need to have all new choir members fill out an information sheet giving you important facts like that.

I also sometimes print a thought for the week or a funny quote. That gives "Choir Notes" some needed personality. From time to time I add some catchy clip art as well. Oh, those creative juices never stop.

We Need Somebody to Paint the Choir Room this Saturday
Managing a team of volunteers requires forethought and patience.

How do you recruit volunteers for the many projects that will confront you? The best way is to pay them! But since that's not one of the options here, let's move on.

Remember that information sheet I just mentioned that you have each new choir member fill out? You want to know much more than their name, address, and birthday. One of the questions on that sheet is this: "What skills or gifts would you be willing to donate to the choir if needed?"

Here's where you create your list of carpenters, seamstresses, painters, electricians, typists, writers, graphic artists, speakers, section leaders, emergency accompanists, cookie bakers, telephoners... Got the picture? It doesn't matter what the skill may be, you will most likely find a need for it in the future.

If you advance to the computer age, you will have that list in your data base ready to call forth at the push of a few buttons. Oh that life were that easy.

Once you identify who might be able to do the job you need doing, you have to ask. Now that may seem obvious, but here is where many fail. Delegating the task is not easy for lots of folks. You may be one of those. If so, learn to let go. Besides, the more people you get working for this organization, the more ownership they will have in it. That's good.

When asking for volunteer help, you need to know that there are some people who just can't say no. They often should, but something in their childhood made them want to be acceptable to everybody. They feel that if they say no to you, then you won't like them. If you don't like them, then you won't let them continue to sing in your choir. If you don't let them sing in your choir, they will cry. They don't want to cry, so they will always say yes.

Those are the kinds of people who often overextend themselves. Their hearts are as big as Mt. Rushmore, but they don't always have the capacity to deliver what you need. Their enemy is time.

I have learned this the hard way. I have encountered some absolutely lovable people who would say yes to do anything I asked of them. But when the play should be over and the curtain falling, I discover at the last minute that the star hasn't even shown up at the theater yet. These have been painful times. You want to avoid them.

So when you do approach someone, evaluate your request. How much time is this going to take? Is that individual really able to take it on?

Then when you ask them, give them an out. Ask them if they honestly feel that they can make the time to do this job for you. Tell them to feel free to say no if they think they should — you'll understand.

By taking that approach, you may save them and yourself from some future anguish. You may in fact be teaching them to say that little word that they needed to learn from childhood — "NO."

Once you have a volunteer recruited, give them your expectation clearly. If you need to have the results completed by the 15th of the month, ask them if they would be willing to get in touch with you for a progress report around the 10th. Put it on your calendar. If they don't call you, you call them.

It's when you become absolutely dependent on certain volunteers that you become vulnerable. If your music librarian is the only person alive who knows how the music library operates, you're headed for trouble. If your children's choir coordinator is the only one who knows the schedule of who's to bring the cookies to rehearsal, you're headed for trouble.

So as you supervise your various volunteers, request reports and updates from them just as if they were employees. Treat them like professionals. Set up regular meetings with them: They will appreciate the opportunity to be heard, even if you don't have the need to hear them.

If the nursery is one of the areas run by your volunteers, be sure to keep close tabs on what goes on there. Out of sight, out of mind. If you don't visit the nursery yourself, you will forget that there's some vital activity going on there. If the volunteers you have in that area are not doing the job right, you need to correct it before it corrects you.

Keep your ear to the ground in the volunteer department. Ultimately you will save yourself from short circuit city.

There's No Place Like Home
Your facility requirements need special care and attention.

That building you call your church is home for your music ministry. You will need to give it some special love and attention.

If you are blessed with a wonderful building with lots of room and equipment, you will be among the elite. Even the newest, most expensive church compounds are notorious for short changing the music department.

But if your facility is all you want it to be, then perhaps the only thing you will need to concern yourself with is how to decorate your rehearsal space so that it takes on colorful personality.

They didn't tell me I would be an interior decorator.

That's no joke. You should take seriously the psychological impact the color scheme has on your choir. You need to be concerned as well with the spiritual focus the room inspires.

Of the many other things we can say concerning this important territory known as the choir rehearsal room, remember that some day you may be in the position of overseeing the remodeling or the initial building of a new facility. Keep some of these criteria for worship and music facilities in mind.

There's the question of convenience and comfort. How is the air flow? Lack of good air circulation in the choir room will kill your rehearsal.

What problems do the people have hanging up their coats? That little inconvenience can be more annoying than you ever dreamed.

What is the lighting like? Some of us have bad eyesight, and we need to have good lighting to read all those little notes playing across those lines. Have you ever sat in the choir's seats and looked to see what the lighting and the background is like for you, the director? If your face is in the shadows, or if the background behind you is too busy, people aren't going to be able to concentrate on your leadership as they ought. They may not even realize why, but it will be a real problem — not imagined.

If the problem is that the room behind you is too busy and distracting, then you might want to try a simple solution that worked for me in one location. We just installed a green window shade that I could pull down right behind me. The choir loved it. That was especially true when someone would sneak into the choir room and put some sort of surprise message on the shade before I arrived. Boys will be boys, you know.

How are the chairs in which the choir members sit? Your singers should be able to sit up straight with a spine consciousness, even on the front edge of the chair. But it is important that they are comfortable in those seats. Those "awful gray metal folding chairs" are just the opposite of what you need.

If you can avoid it, you should never have yourself elevated higher than the singers. In doing that, they have to look up when they sing. That makes it harder for them to see you and see their music at the same time, and it puts an unnatural strain on their throats when they sing.

Ideally you should have tiered seating in your choir rehearsal space. The problem most churches run into with this is that the ceilings are not tall enough to accomodate the risers. When this happens, the poor guys on the back rows get claustrophobic as their hair brushes the ceiling. And its not that the air is thinner there because of height — they aren't that high off the ground — but the air does indeed get thinner at the ceiling level where heat rises. So aim for high ceilings. It helps with the sound, too.

I believe every choir rehearsal room needs a small sound system. You should have good speakers and a good tape deck available for recording the choir for immediate playback and for good quality taped accompaniments. The speakers should be mounted above the heads of the choir, and the equipment should be built into the room, readily accessible.

But there is another use for this equipment that will greatly enhance your rehearsals. Amplify your own voice. Invest in a lavalier microphone to wear during the rehearsals. While people are singing, you will be able to talk above the music and be heard. That enables them to hear you much better and helps save your poor voice from more strain. Just be careful that you don't do too much singing over that microphone yourself. It's tempting to help the altos or tenors along when they are struggling. You may be the last person in the world who should do that. Besides, if you're singing along, you won't be able to hear what the rest of the choir is doing.

Most of what has been said about your rehearsal space can be said about the choir loft. No, I don't believe you should practice the entire time in the choir loft. I believe the choir needs to have its own space for midweek and Sunday morning rehearsals.

The choir loft needs good acoustics, good lighting, good air flow, and comfortable chairs. Don't forget the need to get into and out of the loft easily. I've known churches whose choir usually processed at the beginning of the service. So they built the choir loft with only one way to get into it — walking down the center aisle. That can pose many problems later on, so build in a separate access and exit to the choir loft for times you are not processing.

Nine out of ten churches fail to plan for adequate storage. Even if they think they do, they often end up converting space intended for storage into classrooms or offices later on. So if you ever have the opportunity to design storage space, ask for more than you think you'll need. You will eventually use it.

Many of the items in the music department require climate-controlled storage. Consider, for instance, the choir robes, handbells, the music, electronic equipment and keyboards, tapes, timpani, instruments for the children's choirs, charts for teaching music to the children, costumes, sets, lights, dimmer boards, and paint. Then there still needs to be space for the risers to go somewhere.

Yes, you need lots and lots of storage space. Some of it will need to be near the rehearsal area, but some of it will need to be near the sanctuary instead. And when you do get that space, put a lock on it.

Another place where I've seen churches goof is in the movement of people. You have to get your congregation into and out of that worship area gracefully. Many of them will want to stop in the narthex and the halls to talk to one another after the service. There will often be a desire to set up tables in those same halls to have people sign up for various church activities. So you need to have lots of extra movement space in that narthex and in those halls. Cutting down there to save money will be something you will regret forever.

When you do have the challenging opportunity to improve your own facility, you need to do something very important. You need to visit other facilities to see what worked and what didn't. It is well worth your time and money to go across the country, if necessary, to see the best examples possible of church architecture. That learning experience is worth far more than reading about it as you are here, talking to someone about it over the telephone, or ever trusting an architect to anticipate all your needs accurately.

Where Were You on the Night of August 27th?
Keep a detailed calendar of your activities.

What did we do without calendars? I guess we made scratches on cave walls. You need to fall in love with calendars and accumulate several.

One of them is that calendar you use to plan your music for coming months. That is a very special calendar unto itself. It never leaves your office; or if it does, it never leaves your person. On that calendar you circle in red the first day of Lent, Palm Sunday, Good Friday, Easter, Mother's Day, Father's Day, Independence Sunday, Labor Day, Thanksgiving Sunday, First Sunday in Advent, Christmas Eve, and your wife's birthday.

By the way, it's not a bad idea to put your secretary's birthday on there as well.

Then you have your appointment calendar. This one shows you the week at a glance, and you should be able to break your days down into hours. Whether you keep this calendar or you ask your secretary to do it, everything you do should be recorded on it. Some day the Administrative Committee or the Personnel Committee or the senior pastor is going to ask you to justify this enormous salary you're getting. That calendar will be your diary.

Then you should get a pocket calendar. Carry it with you all the time. Take it to all staff and committee meetings. Take it home so that you and your spouse can have periodic "calendar parties." That's where the two of you get your respective calendars, a pencil or two, and your favorite beverage. You communicate to one another all the things you have to do and all the things you would like to do during the next month or three. And be sure that one of the things you put on that calendar is a date night for you and your spouse. If you don't, all those nights will be taken from you.

Now here is the tricky part. You need to do two things. You need to transfer information from one calendar to another. For instance, when you go to lunch with the committee chairman and he invites you to a breakfast meeting two weeks from Friday, tell your secretary. She'll get fewer gray hairs that way. So will you.

The second tricky part is even more crucial. Read the calendar regularly and show up at breakfast two weeks from Friday. Your future employment may depend on it.

I recently consulted at a church which was examining their whole worship and music ministry. They had just fired their minister of music and were looking for a replacement. My job was to help them evaluate where they had been, where they were, and where they wanted to go as they looked forward to a new beginning.

In hearing from staff people, choir members, and congregational members about the fellow who had just departed, I heard a very common theme. He was loved. He was a decent musician. He was spiritually in tune with the church. But his greatest recurring problem was that he could never get himself organized. He tried to keep calendars because the senior pastor insisted on it, but he failed to consult his calendar. So he often missed appointments, meetings, even weddings. His lack of responsibility was embarrassing to everyone — especially his secretary who tried like crazy to help him remember what day of the week it was.

This lack of administrative ability carried over into the choir's rehearsal each week. The choir would arrive on Wednesday night, never knowing which of the anthems they had been rehearsing would be sung the following Sunday. Often the music for that week was only put into the folders for a maximum of two rehearsals. They would spend 90% of the time that night learning one piece of music for that coming service, putting them further behind as they returned to the same routine the next week.

Many attempts were made to help this fellow through his maze of missed meetings, but to no avail. Finally he was asked to leave.

Learn to love calendars. They will love you.

CHAPTER 9

THEY DIDN'T TELL ME

◆ ◆ ◆

I Would Need To Be A Personality.

The Situation

GREG WAS A MINISTER OF MUSIC IN OHIO. He was very much loved by the people of his congregation. But Greg decided that it was time to move on to greener pastures.

That church job was a very desirable position, one that almost didn't need to be advertised. In fact, the church had over a dozen applications just by word-of-mouth. One of them was an outstanding soloist in the choir, someone who was known to everyone. His name was Kenneth.

Kenneth had two music degrees, was teaching music in high school in the community, and really wanted the job at this church. The committee interviewed him early in the search process, concluding that they really didn't have to audition him because they already knew of his musical abilities. He was, in fact, eminently qualified for the job.

But the committee didn't choose Kenneth. The reason — his dry personality. Greg, you see, was a "people person." He was the life of the party, always "on stage," full of jokes and laughter. There was more to him than that, but his winning ways endeared him to many people. Choir rehearsals were actually fun.

Kenneth was "Mr. Serious." Life for him was something to be analyzed and calculated. He was extremely pleasant, no guile, no enemies. But he was boring. The committee decided that the contrast between the two personalities would be Kenneth's downfall. And even if the obvious contrast were not evident, they were still not convinced that Kenneth would be able to win over the people in the choir.

Kenneth was extremely likable, extremely competent; but he went from job to job over the next few years trying to find those who would appreciate what he had to offer. What he had to offer was considerable, but it was not packaged in an attractive way. If only he could learn to show some enthusiasm for life.

I was attending a concert of an oratorio. The choir was outstanding, the orchestra was superb, and the soloists were top-notch. But of the four soloists, one of them stood out very positively while the other three came up wanting.

It had nothing to do with their singing abilities: All four soloists were highly talented professionals. But the soprano radiated when she sang. Her eyes sparkled with every syllable. Her heart was obviously involved at a very deep level with the meaning of the music, and she sang with undeniable empathy.

The other three soloists looked studied. They never smiled. You could hear the difference in their tone color. Even with my eyes closed, I would have been able to tell that these people were somber and detached. The bass, as a matter of fact, never looked off his score at the audience.

I went backstage after the concert to a reception. I already knew the tenor personally, but I met the other three soloists for the first time. The soprano again was a very confident, positive creature. She was enjoying every minute of life.

The alto likewise surprised me with her radiant personality. I thought to myself that perhaps she was just scared during the performance. What a shame her vitality didn't show then.

Then I met the bass. He looked as if he had just lost his wallet and had no American Express Card. There was no warmth there at all. I wondered if he were ill.

About six months later I ran into a colleague who had hired that bass to sing the role of Elijah in Mendelssohn's great oratorio. I asked him how it had gone.

"Well, he did a very good job. But you know what, he was uninspired. Even in the Baal sequence, while the choir was getting all worked up and Elijah was mocking the priests and all, this guy sort of walked through the score like he was eating cardboard."

I wasn't too surprised to hear that after my own experience, but at least it confirmed what I was thinking.

Then he added, "I picked him up at the airport and took him back. My wife hosted a party afterwards at our home. I was with him a number of

I Would Need To Be A Personality.　　　　　　　　　　　　　　199 ◆

times during the weekend, but it was like he never woke up!"

Alas, that was the best description I had heard of this man's personality. While he can really sing, I wouldn't want to hire him — not even for my funeral.

Tim was a fine organist. But his attitude towards life was so dry that one would imagine him to be an undertaker rather than a church musician.

He loved to play the organ, and he practiced it diligently. Almost every time I would enter the sanctuary during the day while he was practicing, I would find a metronome ticking away right by his side. He would methodically move through every piece of music with that metronome controlling the speed, and it was his favorite form of rehearsal to play sixteenth notes as if they were half notes. Someone had taught him this method of learning Bach, so he applied it to every piece of music he knew.

I was amazed one day to discover him rehearsing "What a Friend We Have in Jesus" with a metronome.

Tim's playing was uninspired. Yes, as I said, he was a fine organist; but his playing was mechanical. Even his choice of registrations were tiring. I believe that if he had been asked to play a piece of romantic music, he would have freaked out.

I had some open conversations with him on several occasions about his view of life, of the Lord, of music, and all the other interesting things that church musicians chew on over lunch. Tim had enough self awareness to admit to me that he didn't like himself very much. I could have guessed he was carrying around that burden, and I suspect that same is true of many other pensive, withdrawn personalities.

Tim desperately needed to loosen up, and he definitely needed counseling for his self-image problem. His wife told me she was considering divorce.

***

It's true. You need some personality to go along with your musical ability and your great love for the Lord. There needs to be some outward, visible evidence of that lovable inner self you know so well.

Think back to your school days. Who were your favorite teachers? Most of them were the ones who made you enjoy learning. Right?

Think about your favorite doctors. Isn't it far more pleasant to get medical care from someone who makes you feel at ease and communicates with you than it is from someone who just says, "Hmmm" every time he pokes?

I am convinced that one of the traits of the best church musicians is an outgoing personality. And those choirs that are the most committed are also the ones that love to laugh.

I'll bet nobody ever told you that you should be a comedian when you direct the choir.

Some Solutions

Come to the Party
Choir rehearsals should be fun!

I LOVE IT WHEN MY CHOIR PEOPLE TELL ME how much they enjoy being in the choir. Consider the alternative. How would you like it if your people came up to you and said, "Choir rehearsal is a real bore, but I make myself do it anyway."? You need that like you need another car repair bill.

I've known situations like that, however, and I find them very gloomy. I've talked with some very dedicated choir members whose lament is that their director is a dud. That's sad.

Choir rehearsals should be fun! That doesn't mean that they are not work. In fact, most choir members will enjoy your rehearsals much more if they are lots of work. They've come there to learn music and do a great job with it. How boring and defeating it is to come and just wade through some music that is offered half-heartedly each Sunday.

Since you, the director, are the lead character in this one-act play each week, you need to set the stage for the atmosphere of the rehearsal.

The attitude with which you begin rehearsal will make a world of difference in what follows. There is such a thing as group psychology. It's a mysterious force that takes over a group of people and seems to clandestinely announce that we are or are not going to enjoy this.

Have you ever noticed your choir arriving for a rehearsal, and it seems that just about everybody's posture is slumping? They aren't smiling, and the general sound in the room is several decibels lower than usual. Well, the Grouch Who Stole Choir Rehearsal was prowling their offices that day, spoiled their dinner, and was roaming the parking lot as they arrived. You have to overcome that, and it begins at the beginning.

I've lost track of how many times I have entered a choir rehearsal with an upset stomach or headache or just general fatigue. If I hadn't been in charge, I would have stayed home. Identify?

Well, in spite of those occasions, you need to be *positive*. Talk yourself into it. More importantly, pray like crazy that the Lord will move by His Spirit over that group in spite of you. He will.

There have been a few times when I've not tried to fake it with my choir. I've told them right out that I was not 100% that night, so would they please try to overlook it and do their thing anyway. They seem to empathize immediately and will rise to the occasion.

There is a wonderful story I love to tell that's applicable here. It has to do with a family who made their living as trapeze artists in the circus. The whole family participated — even the youngest.

A new son was born into the family, and as soon as he was old enough, the father would take him into the circus tent each afternoon and put him on the trapeze for some introductory lessons. Each day the father would raise the height of that trapeze just a little.

The day finally arrived that the dad took this little guy to the top of the rigging. The boy was very surprised to discover that it looked much further down from up there than it had the other way around. He was very nervous.

"Son," the father said, "today you are going to take hold of this bar and swing over to the other side. Then I want you to let go and throw your body through the air and catch that other trapeze over there. Don't worry if you fall: The net below will catch you."

This poor little fellow looked up at his father with wide eyes, looked down at that net below, and then over to the trapeze that seemed so very far away. Fear began to invade every part of him, and he just couldn't move a muscle.

The dad, realizing what his son was experiencing, thought for a moment and then said these very wise words: "Son, don't worry. Just throw your *heart* over that bar, and your *body* will follow."

I love that. There is so much truth to it. On many occasions, whether it's leading choir rehearsal or leading worship on Sunday morning, I find that I have to throw my heart into it just so I can get my tired body to follow.

I Would Need To Be A Personality.

But you know what, I've found that it works in reverse as well. There have been just as many occasions when my body felt fine, but my spirit was just not into it. I would obediently throw my body into the task and then be surprised when I discovered my heart catching up.

The worship and the music of the choir rehearsal and the Sunday morning service have a way of reviving us. But you may have to fake it sometimes just to get started.

How do you begin your rehearsals? I'm not asking now what the style is of your beginning, but what are your routines? People enjoy a certain amount of consistency, so you should consider scratching that itch with the kick-off routine.

I usually have the accompanist start playing some great hymn or worship song. I soon get the choir to join in with the singing. That is a smooth way to help them move from casual conversations upon arriving and into a common focus — worship through music. It helps get their singing mechanisms going. It announces to anyone still not in their seat that it's now time to begin.

I also have a silly little ritual that I fell into years ago, and I've been amused at how my people have grown to expect it and anticipate it. I say in a loud and very positive voice, "Hello, choir!" They respond with a very positive and upbeat, "Hello, Harry." We smile at one another smugly and move on. I guess there's some child in all of us. Besides, that sort of trademark helps people identify and have a sense of belonging.

One last comment before moving on. If you're a bit of a ham, great. Just imagine that your rehearsal is being video taped for later playback. That will spark your attitude.

Look for the Silver Lining
*You need to find humor wherever you can
and interject it as you go.*

Humor is essential to good health. We have long known that laughter has therapeutic value for the human animal. When you laugh, there are certain chemicals that are released in your body. Your brain functions differently. You have more energy. Your immune system is actually improved.

Yes, laughter is healing. And you therefore need to learn how to apply this balm in your work.

Look for comedy wherever you can find it. If it's in the text you are singing, then point it out. If it's in a dumb comment you just made, then allow everybody to laugh at it. If you can think of an off-the-wall way to describe a sound you just heard, then use it. Take the time to laugh together, then move on quickly. You obviously don't want your rehearsal to become a soiree.

Caution: Put your brain into gear before you put your mouth into motion. I have eaten my foot more often at choir rehearsals than I would like to admit because I would try to be funny, but I would instead say something that was too strong. That is especially true when I am trying to get one of the sections to make a better tone. For instance, I once said the first thing that came to my mind (mistake) to the soprano section when they were pinching a high note to death. "Ladies, you sound like a cow that just stepped on her udder!" Yes, there was an uproarious laughter from everybody in the choir — except the females. I was in the area of bad taste, and there were no breath mints strong enough to make us want to kiss and make up. On some occasions I've had to apologize. It was good for me.

The choir loves it when you are secure enough to allow the joke to be on you. They will most love to laugh at you, so long as you are able to laugh along with them. So if you make a funny mistake, laugh at yourself and don't let it bother you if the choir does, too. Those are perhaps the best comedy moments of all.

Subscribe to Reader's Digest
Find some ready-made humor to share occasionally.

If you are not the life of the party, you may need some extra help with this humor thing. When that is the case, you need to look for some humorous stories, cartoons, quotes, and jokes from any source you can.

When you find those gems, cut them out and put them into a file. Always carry a few of them in your choir folder for "emergencies."

When one of those nights comes along in which you are feeling like a morgue and the choir is missing more notes than usual, take a moment between selections and say, "Oh, by the way, I found something here that I thought you'd enjoy." Then proceed to share your pearl with them.

They'll hopefully laugh, adrenalin will kick in, and then they won't miss so many notes.

Bring in the Clowns
Find and cultivate the clowns in your choir.

Every choir has at least one clown. In my experience, the clown is usually a male. I've had more tenor clowns than baritones. I wonder if that's common? Somebody ought to get a government grant and do a study on that.

The choir clown is always full of jokes. He will have a wise crack about every ten minutes. You will quickly spot him, because all the other men sitting around him will suddenly break into unconstrained laughter, stopping all proceedings of the rehearsal momentarily. He will be the one looking at you sheepishly.

That's not necessarily good. You may need to put a lid on those guys so that the rest of the choir doesn't get annoyed with the private jokes that interrupt.

Here's what you do. Get to know your choir clown. Take him to lunch. Befriend him. Let him know that you love his humor and that you believe it is vital to the good health of the choir that he use that God-given talent of his to keep things light in rehearsals when they get too heavy.

I point out that I am prone to get too intense in the rehearsal, wanting to get the best possible results from the choir. Whenever he sees that happening, I would appreciate his lightening up the atmosphere a little.

That permission always caused a look of glee to come from my clown. He thought I was going to clip his wings, and instead I'm inviting him to charge ahead.

Whenever I've done this, my clown would often say to me that he hoped I was not offended when he poked fun at me in front of the choir. My answer is always no, absolutely not. I think the choir's greatest fun is often at the expense of the director. But keep it in good taste, of course.

Then I've added the second most important point of the conversation. I explain that it is naturally easy for the whole thing to get out of hand. We need to remember that the whole choir wants to accomplish as much as possible in the rehearsal. So let's have an agreement. If I sense that he is overdoing it a little and the choir rehearsal is deteriorating as a result, I will give him some sort of secret signal, letting him know to back off.

My clowns have always appreciated that. They have always admitted that their wives sang a constant litany of "You don't know when to quit." Our little secret was just the thing to give him the freedom to be who he was without making me mad in the process.

Say "Cheese"
Get your choir to smile and enjoy themselves more.

You need to employ some conducting ideas that will get the choir involved in playful ways. That's not only for the psychological uplift needed in rehearsals, but it's also important for the best delivery of much of the music they sing.

I'm really turned off by a stilted, bleak, and joyless rendering of a praise chorus or exciting anthem. It's amazing to me that many of those people standing up there in their robes are singing about the most momentous events of the Universe and the most exalted Person of history as if they were reading the white pages of the phone book. Yet those same "worshipers" will go to the stadium or to their television sets that same afternoon and cheer uproariously for their favored team.

Teach your choir to sing from the *heart*. Another one of my favorite quotes is this: "If your heart has found the message, notify your face!"

Here's a suggestion or two. Have the choir members raise their eyebrows. I always get a fun response when I ask them to "raise the real ones *and* the painted ones." Try it right now. Feel the sensation.

Raising the eyebrows lifts the entire face. It opens the eyes more widely which improves the communication of the choir. It naturally brightens the singing tone, placing more warmth into it. And it raises the soft palate in the back of the mouth, causing the throat to open more and thus creating a better sound. All that from just one simple gesture. They look better; they sound better.

You should add a new gesture to your conducting vocabulary — the eyebrows. Practice the Groucho Marx movement. Your choir will respond gleefully.

Sometimes I also tell the choir to lift their cheek bones so that they touch their eyebrows. That's like trying to kiss your elbow, but the response is similar to raised eyebrows.

Have the choir sing what should be an exciting passage from an anthem or song with their eyes closed. You might also suggest that they keep an expressionless face as they sing — one that looks like it's been injected with Novacaine.

Have them listen to the sound. Now sing it again, still with the eyes closed, only this time with a raised-eyebrow lift to the face. They will hear a remarkable difference immediately.

You then tell them that you can not only *see* the difference in their facial communicatin, but you can *hear* the difference as well. Since that's true of the congregation and of the Lord, who is their true audience, they should remember to apply it all the time.

The Shadow of Your Smile
Following a great minister of music takes some careful thought.

Tony was just a little too sure of himself when he followed an outstanding guy in the position of choir director. The man who left the job had built a strong program and had retired after long years of service to the church. Tony was young, bright, and very capable. The church was blessed to find him.

Tony took the job in the fall and announced early on that the selection for his first Christmas on the job would be MESSIAH. People were pleased with the choice. They had done the Christmas portion of Handel's classic a number of times in the past and had always found it satisfying.

But at the first rehearsal where Tony made that announcement to the choir, he made a statement intended to encourage and motivate them. Instead, it built walls. He said, "We are going to present MESSIAH with a Baroque orchestra in the way that Handel intended it. This is going to be the *best* performance of MESSIAH this church has ever had!"

The room froze. There were many, many memories of past Messiah performances when things had gone extremely well. They had used a Baroque orchestra before, including a real harpsichord. For this new guy to say that he would lead them in a way as to surpass his beloved predecessor was insulting to that man's memory. It was a big mistake for Tony to make. Nobody ever told him how to follow a previous minister of music.

You will probably find yourself in the same position as Tony, stepping into the footprints of a minister of music who came before and who had built his own set of loyal disciples. How you handle that will say much about your ability to exercise wisdom.

As most pastors are taught in seminary, when you assume a brand new position, it is wise to wait at least one or two years before you make too many dramatic changes. For instance, if the choir has always rehearsed on Wednesday nights for one hour, you don't want to immediately switch to Thursday nights for two hours. Suppose the choir has always sung a call to worship. Don't eliminate it during your first month on the job. People resist that sort of change, even if you feel you have good reasons for making it.

As you do make changes slowly, remember to affirm everything you can about their past and present way of doing things. If they excel in good tone color, affirm both the choir and your predecessor for the good choral training. If they show a sensitive love for one another in the choir, give credit to those who have gone before you for nurturing that important trait. Don't take for granted that any of those qualities were born naturally.

Never criticize the styles of music that they are used to singing. So you can't stand accompaniment tapes. That doesn't mean that you make a big deal out of it and have a tape burning party right off the bat.

Does this mean that you can't do anything your way during the first two years on the job? Of course not. Be yourself. You are your own personality following a different personality. You will face the mentality from some choir members of "we've never done it that way before." You don't have to apologize for your own creativity or leadership abilities.

I Would Need To Be A Personality. 209

Just love those people where they are and gently suggest that they try this out for size. They just might like it.

Over a period of time — and taking time is one of the crucial points to remember — you will build your own foundation and your own followers. Some may never accept you, especially if your predecessor was their personal friend and pastor; but that does not negate your credentials and viability.

While we are talking about arriving on the scene, you ought to think about the fact that some day you will probably want to leave. Entering a new job has one set of standards that you need to follow; leaving creates yet another whole scene.

Remember that when you leave, your memory will remain. That personality that you will take with you to the next job will linger behind like the smell of sweet perfume or the stench of rotten tomatoes. Hopefully you will be remembered for that attractive aroma.

Don't burn bridges. You may be leaving because the pastor is an alligator out to take your hide. You may be leaving because of the Scrooge mentality of the church board. But no matter how angry you may have become or how hurt you may feel, avoid the desire to go out like the tail of a comet. Yes, you may singe the people you would like to burn, but that will come back to haunt you in the future. Others will be asking about you, seeking a recommendation, or just curiously inquiring about how it went. If you act like a wounded animal when you depart, you will be labeled as one in the future.

Such Knowledge Is Too Wonderful for Me
It is important that you nurture your own positive self image.

When you enter the ministry, you are preparing to give of yourself to others. You are going to be called upon to stretch yourself to the utmost to help others find the best in themselves.

But you are human. You have scars in your past. You have needs, too. Right from the start of your ministry, recognize these human limitations for a healthy understanding of who you are.

The real problem comes when you have a greater need to receive ministry for yourself than you have the capacity to give it to others. You may not even realize it, but others do.

Being willing to accept counseling to improve yourself is a sign of maturity — not weakness. God uses others to build us up, just as He uses us to build others.

One of the most common ailments that the devil likes to use on us is low self image. If you were to guess which is greater — people who *like* who they are or people who do *not* like who they are — which would you guess? The majority of people dislike the person that they have to live with 24 hours a day. They would prefer to be someone else.

There are two Scriptures I would like to share with you that have ministered to many. They speak to this phenomenon of the personality.

The first is Psalm 139. Read and meditate on it. It teaches that God created us. He saw us in our mother's womb before we were born. He knows every day that we will live before we live it and every word we will speak before we utter it. "Such knowledge is too wonderful for me, too lofty to attain," says the psalmist.

God has created you to be exactly who He wants you to be. You are created in His image according to His perfect wisdom. So what if your nose is on the side of your head. So what if your earthly father had so many problems that he made you feel wormy. God is greater than all those feelings.

The second Scripture is found in I Samuel 10:5-7. There the prophet Samuel is anointing Saul to be the first king of Israel. But notice what Samuel tells Saul he is to do before he takes on this important task.

> "After that you will go to Gibeah of God, where there is
> a Philistine outpost. As you approach the town, you will meet a
> procession of prophets coming down from the high place with
> lyres, tambourines, flutes and harps being played before them,
> and they will be prophesying.
> The Spirit of the Lord will come upon you in power, and
> you will prophesy with them; and you will be changed into a
> different person.
> Once these signs are fulfilled, do whatever your hand
> finds to do, for God is with you.

Hallelujah! The Spirit of the Lord came upon the man Saul and *changed him into a different person*. And when did that happen? When he heard the *music* of the worshipers.

God can do that today. No matter how inadequate you feel — or actually are — for the calling of God on your life, He can send His Spirit to change you. He can equip you for whatever the task.

Remember how Moses felt when God told him to go into Egypt? But look what a difference that obedience produced!

So your personality may need a little tune up. Let the Master Mechanic have a hand at it!

CHAPTER 10

THEY DIDN'T TELL ME

◆ ◆ ◆

I Would Have To Be A Disciplinarian.

The Situation

C **LARENCE IS A LOVABLE GUY.** He's also a little more than overweight, and he loves to laugh. If anybody ever fit the description "Everybody loves a fat man," Clarence does.

Doris was the choir director of the church, and Clarence was one of the tenors. That's putting it mildly: Clarence was the *lead* tenor in the section of four. Without him, the other tenors might as well sit in the soprano section, because the only thing they could sing was the melody.

Doris was grateful to have Clarence singing with them, and the choir was grateful for his voice as well. But Clarence had two very annoying problems: He was always late, and he often failed to show up at all.

By late, I mean that Clarence would walk in after a third of the rehearsal was over! On Sunday mornings, he usually didn't make the rehearsal at all — he would just scramble to get his robe on and hope to get into the lineup with the other three tenors before the choir entered the choir loft.

Several of the altos used to get really annoyed with Clarence and his lack of punctuality. So they took it upon themselves to try to do something about it. Their method was to make comments to him as he would crawl through their section to his assigned tenor seat. Everyone in the choir could hear them. "Nice of you to join us tonight, Clarence." Or sometimes they would say, "Gee, Clarence, aren't you early tonight? You've only missed three anthems."

Jolly old Clarence just let it roll off his back. He would chuckle in his charming fat-bellied way, and all the rest of the guys in the choir would just catcall, "Yeah, Clarence, where you been?"

Poor Doris didn't know whether to laugh or cry. She loved the guy, she needed his music reading ability and lovely voice, but she could feel her blood pressure rise with each repeated offense.

**

Allen is the minister of music of a small church in Florida. It's a good choir, partly because Allen attracted a significant number of students from the music department of the community college nearby.

If you were to ask one of Allen's choir members what time choir rehearsal begins, they would pause and then say, "Around 7:30. But we never start then."

You see, the people in Allen's choir don't get there on time. Oh some do. There are a significant number of very faithful members who are there and in their seats before 7:30 p.m. every week. But they just sit and talk to one another, waiting for Allen to decide when there are enough people present to begin.

Allen is always on time, too. But he just waits. Week after week, it's the same routine. He starts about 7:45 or so — when enough people have arrived, in his opinion.

Sadly, he will often say something about the fact that he wishes everybody would make an effort to get there by 7:30 p.m. next week so that they wouldn't lose valuable rehearsal time. But nothing ever changes.

*
* *

I've heard the same answer to this question countless times.

Question: "How many people do you have in your choir this year?"

Answer: "Oh, about 45. But at Christmas, we run between 65 and 70!"

Whenever I hear that, I cringe. Why are there more people at Christmas? Because singing the Christmas music is fun. It's like a party, and people like to party.

I call those people party crashers. You can bet that you will encounter them. And not just at Christmas, either. If you do an Easter musical, some of these same "friends of the choir" will show up again.

A good number of them will even come to Wednesday rehearsals for a few months because of the Christmas music, and then they won't show up to sing with the rest of the choir on Sunday mornings. What nerve.

*
* *

I've had several great music librarians. They do all the work of numbering the music when it arrives, sorting it, passing it out to the singers in an orderly fashion, taking it back up, checking it for rips, Scotch taping it back to health for future use, putting it back in numeric order, and filing it away again.

Theirs is a thankless job, taken for granted. Thank you, thank you, all of you who take on this marvelous task for your choir. May your days on earth be prolonged and your crown in heaven be more lovely.

None of these music librarians likes every aspect of the job, but there is one thing they all have in common — one pet peeve that sends their sweet spirit into teeth-grinding. They *hate* it when choir members don't turn in their music after it's sung.

Now it's one thing when one or two persons occasionally forget or when someone is out of town and unable to comply. But the fact is that a significant number of the choir members walk away on Sunday mornings, blithely ignoring that someone has to go behind them and find that music. It means counting and sorting to determine who the culprits are. Then it means going into 10 or 20 folders to find the one title that is needed. Then it means more sorting to get those 10 or 20 into numerical order with the others. Then and only then may the music find its final resting place on the library shelf. Multiplied by the number of offenders, the final result can add hours of unnecessary time to the music librarian's task.

As my choir librarians have complained about this to me over and over in the past, I hear a common description: "These people are as bad as kindergartners! They have to have their hand held to do everything! Why don't they shape up?!"

You may place there a voice inflection of total aggravation. I don't blame them. The adults in your choir will indeed often act like children, and you will indeed often feel like you have to become a schoolmaster to keep them in line.

Well, children do need discipline.

As James tells us, the tongue is an uncontrollable part of the human body. Every choir is subject to ultimate demise by the power of the tongue.

One very subtle way that the tongue causes conflict is by people simply talking in rehearsals when they should be listening. It's common. It's annoying. You will face it, and it will be up to you to do something about it.

But there is obviously a greater danger lurking there, ready to pounce upon your choir family. That's the tongue of the complainer, the gossiper, the backbiter.

Rest assured, that temptation will find its mark on someone or a group of someones in your choir.

It only takes one. And that one can start a forest fire of problems for you. Their little asides, their outright criticism of your ministry in the ears of others will be poison. That poison can kill. The devil knows that, and you can be certain he will use it if he can.

What might they complain about? The field is wide open, but here are some interesting examples.

They might attack the fact that some members of the choir are late, and you are allowing them to get away with it.

They might attack the fact that some of the people singing in the choir right now have been allowed to join the choir only to sing the Christmas music.

They might join with the music librarian in condemning the childish behavior of those who fail to turn in music all the time.

They might get hung up on the fact that so many people in the choir are talking when they should be listening, and you continue to let them.

They might even be the very person to denounce the fact that someone else in the choir is a complainer.

Oh, my dear friend, if no one has ever told you this before, let me do so. If you are going to be a minister of music, you are also going to have to learn to be a loving disciplinarian.

Some Solutions

MAKE NO MISTAKE ABOUT IT, God has ordained discipline in our lives. He Himself disciplines us, and He expects us to exercise wise and loving discipline with others as well.

Granted, there is more concern for discipline in our personal lives and in the lives of our families than there is within any organization of the church. But that does not preclude discipline in the church. In fact, the church is one of the few places in our society where good discipline ought to be a prominent, positive example.

It is sadly true in America that commitment is an unpopular word. To be committed is too inconvenient. It doesn't go along with our fast-food, entertainment-oriented mentality. Look at our divorce rate. Does that witness to an attitude of commitment?

We who profess a belief in Jesus Christ as Savior, do we also profess a real commitment to Him as Lord? According to the Scriptures, the answer is no. There are many who want the salvation gift, but they don't want the obligations and sacrifices that go with it.

In the church of Jesus Christ, commitment should be paramount. That automatically requires discipline, which means there is also a need for accountability. Commitment — discipline — accountability.

Consider some of these words of our Father.

> Blessed is the man whom God corrects;
> so do not despise the discipline of the Almighty.
>
> Job 5:17

> Blessed is the man you discipline, O Lord,
> the man you teach from your law.
>
> Psalm 94:12

> The fear of the Lord is the beginning of knowledge,
> but fools despise wisdom and discipline.
>
> Proverbs 1:7

> He will die for lack of discipline,
> led astray by his own great folly.
>
> Proverbs 5:23

> He who heeds discipline shows the way to life,
> but whoever ignores correction leads others astray.
>
> Proverbs 10:17
>
> Whoever loves discipline loves knowledge,
> but he who hates correction is stupid.
>
> Proverbs 12:1
>
> No discipline seems pleasant at the time, but painful. Later on, however, it produces a harvest of righteousness and peace for those who have been trained by it.
>
> Hebrews 12:11

Well, it wasn't intended for this discussion to get so heavy, but this subject is certainly one that deserves that kind of attention.

My conviction is that you need to learn to apply loving, consistent discipline to your music ministry — especially to your choirs. I have discovered over and over that a choir that enjoys that kind of leadership is far happier than one that is allowed to get away with all its bad behavior.

The properly disciplined choir is a loved choir, and they know it. Their morale is higher than those choirs that meander through the motions of worship and music.

Here's the Line. Don't Cross It.
Set expectations for your choir that they understand and can live with.

When I assumed one of my past jobs, the choir had already set the policy of electing choir officers. These persons had met, and they were dominated by the secretary of the group whose name was Charlotte.

Charlotte had been a school teacher in her past. She wasn't as young as she used to be, and her tolerance level for little ones was diminishing. I believe she tended to see the adults in the choir in the same light. As I said, adults can act very childishly at times.

Charlotte had convinced the officers of the choir to set up "Rules of Choir Membership." They were good rules, excellently written. I couldn't have asked for better guidelines if I had authored them myself.

I Would Need To Be A Disciplinarian.

But the complaint was that people were violating those rules. Something had to be done by me to pull those offenders back into line.

I stumbled around a bit with how to handle this situation, and it actually took me a long time to come up with the best answer. What I am about to share with you really works — if you just apply it.

I took my choir on an all-day Saturday retreat. That was an annual tradition that the choir learned to anticipate with great joy. I never shared with them before each retreat what the theme of the day would be, just that there were indeed plans with an expected outcome.

In addition to some musical rehearsal on Christmas music and some really fun times of getting to know one another better, I gradually allowed my theme to unfold. Using several Biblical passages to affirm the greatness of God and our call to love Him with our whole being, I easily led the group to agree that we should ideally give Him only our best. That's a little like motherhood and apple pie, you know. Who was going to disagree with that?

I then divided the choir into small groups with a discussion assignment. Each group was to elect a spokesman who would take notes on their discussion and then later report back to the total group. Their question was, "If you had no fear of failure, what do you believe this choir ought to do in order to be the best choir it can possibly be for Jesus Christ?"

I put in the phrase about fear of failure because that is the one most common immobilizer of all. We often fail to even try, simply because we are afraid we will fail.

Well, the answers came back. They were somewhat predictable, but I responded as if each one was a fresh, new idea. For some people, that was true: They had never thought of these things before.

We gathered the information as it was shared and put it on large newsprint all around the room. Each group had its own newsprint representing the written minutes of their individual meeting.

Here are the kinds of things they said.

- We should all show up to rehearsals and be on time.
- We should all participate in all choir activities, including special rehearsals.
- We should not talk during rehearsals, but should give our full attention to what is going on.
- We should mark our music with our pencils whenever instructions are given.
- We should get to know one another better (as they were doing that day) and pray for one another regularly.
- We should all seek to learn to read music.
- We should willingly memorize music more often.

By now you have the picture. I could have just collected the data that day and patted everyone on the back for their great insight. Had I done that, we would have fallen back into the former routines. There would have been no measurable growth.

Instead, I commended them; but I added, "These ideas are so good, that I am going to ask your elected choir officers to take them and study them. Then I want the choir officers to come back to you on a rehearsal night — say in about two weeks — with their written recommendations on what we should adopt as our official policy. We'll all vote on it after we've had another chance for discussion."

But that was not all. "One important thing I think we should all recognize. These ideas will only work if there is some kind of *accountability* built

I Would Need To Be A Disciplinarian.

in. If you say that someone needs to be at rehearsal, what is his responsibility to that? Does that mean he has to be at absolutely all rehearsals, or can he miss sometimes? And what happens if he does miss? Is there any accountability there? I want the officers to make proposals to you on those questions as well as to respond to your ideas."

I don't think they were expecting that, but it made sense. After all, they had spent lots of time and energy reinventing the wheel that day, so doing something proactive with the information seemed like a good idea.

Notice that I emphasized that these were *their* ideas. They were. I could have written them myself, but it was the choir members who actually generated the lists.

Later I met with the officers. In that meeting I reiterated my request to them and clarified it. Then I asked them to do something which I considered very important. I asked them to give their report a new name. Instead of calling it "Rules for Choir Membership" as they had in the past, I asked them to use a more positive name, one that was less likely to elicit rebellion. The name I proposed was "Expectations for Excellence." They loved that idea, and it stuck.

The meeting came. The elected representatives of the choir fed back to the choir members their *own* data for what they should do to reach for excellence. There were no objections voiced in the discussion, and the plan was adopted.

Had I written that document and presented it as what I wanted to see happen, many would have rebelled. Had the choir officers been the collective author, the same thing would have happened.

I have been all over America teaching in conferences and leading choir retreats in Churches. Probably 75% of the choir directors I have had the privilege of meeting have asked me to give them specific feedback on attendance issues for the choir rehearsal. While my specifics may not be exactly what will work best in your circumstances, I'll share them with you here. Just remember that it is universally true — when these "Expectations for Excellence" are lovingly and consistently exercised, the choir flourishes. It even increases in size! People love a well-oiled machine.

Here are the specifics that are related to attendance and tardiness:

1. There is no such thing as an "unexcused" absence in our choir. Whenever a person needs to be absent, they must take

the responsibility to contact their choir shepherd in advance to state their need to be away. No excuse need be given — it's the step of communication and accountability that's crucial.
2. A person may elect to be absent during the choir year (school year) for three times — no questions asked. If more than three absences are needed, the choir shepherd will determine if the excuse is adequate. (This is included to cover extended sicknesses, pregnancies, business men who travel, long vacations to Europe, and those types of things. It is not there to cover fatigue or extra work load at the office. Those things happen, but commitment means that we can count on you to be there *sacrificially* if necessary.)
3. Unexcused tardiness is not tolerated. If a person does find it necessary to be late, they need to contact their shepherd in advance. If they were late due to a slip-up or an emergency, they need to communicate the same way. If one is late three times, that constitutes one of their three absences a year.

Here comes one of the more fun statements associated with all of this: We live under grace, not under law. Isn't that wonderful?

People will stumble in their commitments on these and other issues. That's when we want to exercise grace. These Expectations are not enforced in a police fashion, but in a brother-and-sister fashion. My shepherds monitor the situation well. If they discover a choir member who is consistently failing, or if they uncover an attitude problem in one of the singers, they contact that person and seek to talk about it. That's where their own listening skills are so important.

When there is an ongoing delinquent in the choir, then it's my turn to be the bad guy. I meet with them and seek to be understanding, but I point out that their commitment to the choir needs to be reexamined. If they don't feel that they can subscribe to our "Expectations for Excellence" before the Lord, then I would suggest to them that perhaps God has not called them to this particular ministry. Go and find their calling.

Do my choir members cooperate 100% with this approach? Of course not. But I can truthfully say that by raising the standard high, the vast majority of the choir members do indeed alter their behavior and attitudes. The term "commitment" is no longer a dirty word, and the morale of those who are on board is high.

One Rotten Apple
What do you do with that rebel who makes waves?

The Complainer in the choir may also end up being your primary rebel. He or she will use their tongue to lash out, partly because he or she is under conviction.

You see, when we have rebellion in our heart, God knows it, and so do we. When we begin to feel rebellious, yet we are surrounded by others who are not, we come under conviction. If we are being reminded constantly of the right road to travel, yet we want to take another route, we come under conviction. The Spirit of God speaks in a still, small voice that our spirit recognizes. Then we want to run from the light.

It's in that running that we begin to complain. We begin to try to tear down that which we actually love. It's a paradox.

When someone is caught in that cycle, your job is to love them. That means that you must pray for them. Then you must go to them, take them by the hand, and listen.

Tough love sometimes means that you have to give honest feedback to them. They need to hear from you that while you respect them as a person, you can't allow them to continue to act as they are acting. It damages the spirit of the choir, and it wounds the Body of Christ.

But even before you get to that hard part, most of the time you end the meeting with reconciliation and hugging. That is one beautiful feeling. You will miss it unless you have the courage and take the first steps toward that person — that one sheep who's strayed away from the rest.

Don't say that nobody ever told you how hard this can be, because I'm telling you now.

How Do You Get Into This Outfit Anyway?
Establish a clear means for people to become members of your choir.

One of the worst things you can do to the morale of your choir is allow or even encourage party crashers. When people want to join the choir in November or December just to sing the Christmas music, tell them no.

I know that some of you really want to swell your ranks for that big bash. It strokes your ego a little, and it makes you look good in the eyes of the congregation to have such a large choir up there singing "Silent Night."

But just remember, most (if not all) of those party crashers will be leaving you in January. You will suddenly drop back down to your former size, and I can assure you that the result will be discouragement.

Your choir members will probably have loved the euphoria of singing with more voices a few weeks earlier, but they will find themselves resenting those who have abandoned ship. I've counseled repeatedly with ministers of music who are fighting depression in January. When this situation is the reason, it's their own fault.

I'm sure some of you will say, "But when those people join my choir for Christmas, I almost always get some of them to stay into the new year. So it's a great way to help my choir grow."

You are lying to yourself, my friend. Yes, you may grow by a few persons, but you will shrink in morale nevertheless.

To avoid all of this nonsense, I advocate that you establish a New Choir Member Orientation Class. No one is allowed to just walk in the door and announce that they are joining the choir. *No one.* Instead, each person who is interested in exploring the *possibility* of singing in your choir must first attend that class.

Offer the class in the fall just before the choir season gets under way. You will need to advertise it weeks in advance and require people to *preregister* for it. By raising the standard to that level, you will actually create a greater desire among people to come. It's like the phenomenon of charging for something — you could have just given it away for free, but then people wouldn't want it.

You should lead that class, and invite your key choir leaders to participate in it with you. It lasts about two hours and covers three general topics:

1. What is the role and importance of the choir in worship and music?

2. What are the "Expectations for Excellence" in this choir?

3. What are the normal routines in this choir for a typical rehearsal night and a typical Sunday morning?

Through this process your potential new choir members get to know you, get to know each other before their first rehearsal, get to know some of the other choir members through the leadership represented there, and have a full understanding of what is expected of them *before* they get involved.

I always tell my potential members that there is only one good reason to join the choir, and that is because God *called* them to a ministry of *worship* through music. Furthermore, if they are truly called, they won't have any problem with being at rehearsals, being on time, etc.

What a difference this type of orientation makes for the person who is about to jump onto your moving train. When they come to that first rehearsal, they are far more comfortable than they would have been otherwise.

Did you notice that I kept referring to them as "potential" choir members? I simply tell them that I consider their coming to the first choir rehearsal as a way of testing the waters. I believe it takes the average new choir member three weeks of rehearsals and Sunday services to get into the groove. I suggest to them that they go through those three weeks and then ask themselves if they are comfortable. If so, then perhaps they are called to this ministry; if not, then perhaps God has something more exciting for them to do and they should therefore move on with dignity.

Now this meeting is held in late August or early September. That's the last opportunity for anyone to join the choir until after Christmas. You then repeat the process in January and, if you have the need, again in May for the summer months.

Living under grace and not under law, I have indeed allowed people to join the choir later if they had to miss the Orientation Class. But they may do so only after having a private meeting with me (with the same contents as the class). And — very important — they may never join the choir after a certain cutoff date that is widely publicized in the choir and in the church's publications. For Christmas, that cutoff date is usually mid-October. No more party crashers!

I Think I Can, I Think I Can
Make your choir rehearsals stimulating and challenging.

You will be working with nonprofessionals. If you went to college and sang in a glee club or chorale, you will find the contrast like diamonds and rhinestones. Your amateur choir will indeed be capable of great things, just like the little steam engine that tried to climb the mountain; but it will be up to you to get them to the top!

There are three areas that will take some special attention. Below I'll try to help you with some tricks of the trade that will show improvements in those three areas.

Here's Number One: Someone has said that the average memory span of the typical church choir is five minutes! You will sometimes discover that to be a generous estimate. So your job will be to train your choir for a much better retention rate. They can do it.

Here's how. Give them a pencil. Train them to mark in their music *everything* you say about the interpretation of the composition. That means that if they are a bass, and you're telling the sopranos to sing a rounder "O" in the word "Lord," they will mark that vowel in their bass line as well.

The pencil should be in their writing hand at all times — not in their folder, not in their shirt pocket, not behind their ear, and definitely not in their purse. As a problem spot goes by, circle it. As a breath point is conducted, mark it. As a dynamic expression is asked for, notate it.

From time to time you should plan on having a music-marking session. Before rehearsal, you go through some of the titles you are preparing and mark in all those things that you would guess your singers are going to either miss or on which they are likely to have a difference of opinion. Then announce: "Take your pencils please, and let's put in some markings on this one." That will help train them to keep that pencil handy because

I Would Need To Be A Disciplinarian.

they will never know when you are going to require it.

And one little thing you should do: Provide a pencil sharpener in the choir room. An electric one would be ideal.

Those markings will get you through the next five minutes. They might even get you through Sunday morning. And when you repeat that anthem next year, they will be a tremendous time saver.

Here's Number Two: They will love to talk while you are talking. The moment you stop singing, the choir members are going to start giggling and sharing with their neighbor how many notes they missed that time around. Or they will start having little private rehearsals in their huddle of two — "Sing that for me. How does it go?" In the best cases, they will be commenting on how much they like this piece; in the worst cases, they will be tearing it to shreds. Your job will be to keep their attention on what you are trying to accomplish.

The best way I know to solve that problem — other than a whip and a chair — is to keep the rehearsal pace so alive that they don't have time to talk. Before you stop them while rehearsing a passage, know what you are going to say. Start saying it before the last sound has had a chance to die out. If you are going to have them repeat that passage, move on immediately — no hesitation.

Two things about this pace that you will need to know. The first is that you must find a pace that is fast enough to keep them moving, but not so frantic that they are out of breath by the middle of the rehearsal. That is always a challenge for me: I tend to move so fast sometimes that they don't know what page I'm on. I've learned to control that better over the years. The second is that your accompanist must be in step with you. Train your accompanist to think ahead, just as you are trying to do. The moment the accompanist knows where you are going to be starting in the music again, he or she should be giving the pitches. Lots of time is lost in choir rehearsals waiting for the accompanist to do their thing.

Here's Number Three: Your choir will tend to be lazy and lack self-discipline, if you allow it. Members of your choir will not concentrate. They will tend to view the choir rehearsal as recreation — a night out of the house. They will also be tired, so whatever is happening had better be plenty stimulating for them to want to give of themselves to it.

There are many elements related to the correction of this attitude, but my favorite is this: Have the choir memorize as many selections as possible.

That will not only increase their concentration factor, but it will greatly improve their communication of the music in the worship services. The art of singing is, after all, an art of communication. Teach them that principle, and point out that their art is both aural and visual.

To get a choir to memorize their music, try this plan. Announce to them in the fall (that's when they are fresh and ready to charge) that during the coming year we are gong to attempt to memorize one anthem a month. You will see a mixed reaction: Some will be in the "Hooray" category while others will be saying with their eyes, "Let me outta here!"

Add that you are sure they can do it, and that it won't be difficult at all. You are going to start with some easy choices.

Then pick as your first outing an anthem that is so simple to memorize, it could almost be done in one rehearsal. One choice might be to do a hymn arrangement that is familiar territory. They will probably already know the words that are involved; it will just be a matter of remembering those points where the arrangement detours from the original. I've been known to pick unison or two-part arrangements for this first time out. That makes it even easier for them to succeed.

Success breeds success. If you can get them to succeed rather painlessly the first time around, you will be able to say to them encouragingly, "See! That wasn't so hard!"

The "Hooray" folks will still be cheering; the "Let-me-outta-here" crowd will be relieved, but still skeptical. Now it's round two.

For your second anthem, do the same as before and keep it very simple. In fact, all during the first year of this exercise, increase the challenge only slightly. Make sure that they will succeed by the careful choices you make.

In the spring, announce to them that the following year they will be attempting to memorize two anthems a month. After that, it will increase to three. After they have had three years' experience with this, they will have sharpened their skills so much and will have tasted the joys that singing from memory brings to the point that most of them will love arriving at the final plateau — memorizing everything!

This will all require the firm, gentle hand of a disciplinarian. It will also require developing the quality that many choir members need the most — self discipline.

Have fun, and watch it bear wonderfully good fruit!

Postlude

I'VE BEEN BLESSED WITH SOME absolutely wonderful experiences. Like everybody else, I've also been through the school of hard lessons. Such is life.

My hope is that your learning experiences along the way will be a little more enlightened because of what I've shared here. Perhaps they will even go more smoothly for you than they would have otherwise.

There are certainly other "things" in this career choice that could be examined. Perhaps we'll do that in the future. But as you waltz through the years, just remember that you will never stop growing. Growth is fulfilling, but sometimes a little painful. Expect both.

Help others along the way. We are an elite group, you know. And the devil hates it when we are successful.

I believe you should expect your church to financially support you with at least two weeks every year to get away for seminars and workshops for your personal growth. Most of the time you will want to attend conferences that are dedicated to the musical questions you have to answer daily. But also look around for growth opportunities in some of these other areas when you are considering what workshops to attend. You need to be well-rounded in your quest for excellence.

I enjoy being a minister of music. I'm called to it and fulfilled by it. You are, too, or you wouldn't be where you are. Let's rejoice together for this wonderful privilege of leading others to draw closer to God.

Thank you, Lord, for giving me this privilege. I knew it would be fun, but they didn't tell me it would be this much fun! Amen.

About the Author

REV. C. HARRY CAUSEY began serving in churches as an organist and choir director when still in high school. Through nine years of higher education after high school, the Lord led him to serve a number of different churches of various denominations. He was then called into full-time Christian ministry in 1969, serving for twelve years as minister of music for College Hill Presbyterian Church in Cincinnati, Ohio, and then Fourth Presbyterian Church in Washington, D.C.

He was ordained as a minister in 1980 and in 1981 became a free-lance minister of music, living in Rockville, Maryland, with his wife, Elizabeth, and their two children, David and Debbie. His activities have been varied, leading him to write, compose for the church choir, teach in workshops all over the country, and do consultation for various church music ministries.

In 1983 he founded MUSIC REVELATION, an organization that seeks to minister to today's ministers of music. MUSIC REVELATION publishes a monthly newsletter which is both informative and inspirational. There is also a monthly choral music review service called The Music Review Club. Either or both of these services are on a subscription basis.

Through MUSIC REVELATION, he has also released a number of practical teaching tapes with titles such as "What Is Worship," "How Does God Reveal Himself through Music," "Open the Doors to Creativity in Worship," "How to Improve Your Congregational Singing," "How to Increase the Size of Your Choir," and "How to Take Your Choir on Tour — Happily."

An extended project called FAMILY WORSHIP AT CHRISTMAS consists of a cassette tape and a booklet designed to help your family and those in your church keep Jesus Christ as the focus of the entire Christmas season. This product is available both through MUSIC REVELATION and from Word, Inc.

His first full book is entitled *OPEN THE DOORS... To Creativity in Worship*. Originally released by Valley Press in Washington, DC, it is now in a revised edition and available only through MUSIC REVELATION. This book has found a great following in churches of all sizes and denominations, and it is being used by a number of colleges and universities to train their students who are preparing for a career in church music.

In 1984 the Lord led Rev. Causey to establish The National Christian Choir in Washington, DC. This 250-voice auditioned choir is interdenominational and is seeking to proclaim the glory of God throughout our nation and indeed the world. Not only have they had many concert appearances in Washington at places such as The Kennedy Center, Constitution Hall, The Washington Convention Center, and the National Cathedral, but they have made several recordings with plans to release many more.

You may contact Harry Causey for further information on his ministry, the offerings of his books and tapes, or subscription information concerning MUSIC REVELATION and The Music Review Club. To do so, just write...

MUSIC REVELATION
7 Elmwood Court
Rockville, Maryland 20850-2935
(301) 424-2956